MW00681758

the 52nd poem

a novel

the 52nd poem

a novel by

THOMAS TROFIMUK

Copyright © 2002 Thomas Trofimuk

Great Plains Publications
420 – 70 Arthur Street
Winnipeg, MB R3B 1G7
www.greatplains.mb.ca

All rights reserved. No part of this publication may be reproduced or transmitted in any form or in any means, or stored in a database and retrieval system, without the prior written permission of Great Plains Publications, or, in the case of photocopying or other reprographic copying, a license from CANCOPY (Canadian Copyright Licensing Agency), 6 Adelaide Street East, Suite 900, Toronto, Ontario, Canada, M5C 1H6.

Great Plains Publications gratefully acknowledges the financial support provided for its publishing program by the Government of Canada through the Book Publishing Industry Development Program (BPIDP); the Canada Council for the Arts; the Manitoba Department of Culture, Heritage and Citizenship; and the Manitoba Arts Council.

Design & Typography by Gallant Design
Photography by Gary Nylander
Printed in Canada by Kromar Printing

CANADIAN CATALOGUING IN PUBLICATION DATA

Main entry under title:

Trofimuk, Thomas
The 52nd poem

ISBN 1-894283-31-7

I. Title. II. Title: Fifty-second poem.
PS8589.R644F53 2002 C813'.54 C2002-910091-7
PR9199.3.T675F53 2002

For Leah Fowler, my closest stranger, who said:
"Writers write. If you want to be a writer, just act like one."

And for my rock, Cindy-Lou, and my pebble,
Marie Mackenzie.

prologue

prologue

Perhaps there is a nun named Domonique who hovers only at the edge of this story. You will almost meet her in the mountains but that's later. Much later. You don't have to concern yourself with that meeting. It's a meeting that has the potential to change your life but you're about to begin your relationship with Domonique right now. Open the newspaper. Go on. There, in Section B, on page 3, bottom right hand corner. It's a small story. Read the headline: Nuns 1, Moose 0. You love small stories like this. This one was likely picked up off the wire and placed as a filler. Sometimes stories like this one are gems of bizarreness. Sometimes they rip your heart out. You'll need more light to read this story. Turn on the lamp, over in the corner. There. That's better. This is a story about a carload of nuns who run into a one tonne moose in Ontario and come through unscathed. The moose had to be destroyed at the scene. The story doesn't presume to suggest that God was looking out for the nuns—it just reports the facts—but you start to decipher the story that's stranded in between the lines. You start to wonder what that scene must have been like. Is there a benediction for moose?

Lean back in your chair and think about nuns for a moment. What do you know of nuns? Stereotypes? Habits? Singing? Flying?

Perhaps you can see her in the back seat of the car—her head propped against the window? An unconcerned smile on her face. A flop of hair reveals only half her face. Her skin is smooth and gray in the dim light. But this sleeping nun could be anyone. It's so dark in the car she could be anyone you know. She sleeps as the kilometres drift by. Leaning her head against the cool window and listening to the vibration of the road is a gentle memory from her childhood. Where was she going on those childhood journeys? At journey's end, was her father there to carry her from the car to her bed in a seamless dreamy haze?

Outside, the country flows on and on and on. And Domonique sleeps.

This carload of nuns is headed west with a purpose. They're on the Trans-Canada just across the Manitoba border into Saskatchewan. They're playing a Mozart CD. There are stars clustered between clouds. The hum of the tires on the highway. A dim green light from the dash. And three deer in the ditch. The deer look up. Become frozen dark statues, eyes ablaze.

Pull back. Pull back and away. Can you see the land? The curve of the Earth? What time is it? Can you see the car as it zooms through the darkness, pulled by its own pool of light?

Perhaps you are wondering why she became a nun? You don't have any experience with nuns, especially nuns so young. An older nun once winked at you in a line-up at a grocery store. She was buying four chocolate bars. She winked at you when she noticed you noticing her purchase. It wasn't like you'd caught her buying three 26s of rum. You'd caught her being normal. A nun with a sweet tooth.

But why would a young woman like this become a nun? So much life to experience and she chooses this narrow path. You have no answers. Perhaps when she was five, she knew. Perhaps she knew all her life that this was what she was going to do. There was no question. And now she is a nun, sleeping in a car full of other nuns, on her way across Canada. Or maybe she came to this way of living only recently. Perhaps life itself pushed her into a nunnery.

Oh, my…your fondness for opera is showing. You're writing an opera in your head, for this carload of nuns. It had to be something horrible like her lover dying tragically. But she is dreaming. There are clues inside the subconscious.

Domonique is dreaming that she is floating effortlessly on her back in a vast pool of water. It's warm. There's a faint sulphur smell. The light is dim but she seems to be in a cave. Something's dripping behind her, farther in. A steady distant plinking. She is not afraid. Even though Domonique knows she is claustrophobic, she is not afraid. Her breathing does not quicken or become shallow with fear. She's calm.

She remembers seeing her mother being born. She remembers seeing her mother take her first few gulping breaths. But how can that be? She could not have seen her mother being born. That was before…it's got to be somebody else. How can you remember the birth of someone who was born before you? Yet, she knows in her heart this memory is of her mother.

"But I was born," she says into the darkness. "I was born, and then I crawled, and then I spoke, and then I walked."

Her words flip back to her: "spoke… walked …born… crawled…I…then…"

"No," she whispers. "Born first. Then I crawled. Then I spoke. And then I walked."

"crawled…born…walked…spoke…born…and then…and then…"

"No!"

"Oh!" comes the echo.

She closes her eyes, presses her chest towards the unknown ceiling, pulls shoulders back, floats and breathes, tests her buoyancy, breathes and floats, feels the drift of her hair in the water. Is that a heartbeat?

What can I remember? I loved. I must have loved. I must have been loved. Yes, there are faces and voices in my memory. I love these people. I loved these people. And there is a love, one love, which I denied. I think I turned away because I was afraid. I was terrified. Was this person dying? I forced myself to back away. I stayed safe. And I felt pain. I spent silent days in a bathtub drinking wine out of a tin cup and crying. What does the order of these events matter? Only the things matter. Love and denial and safety. And then pain. Perhaps the pain came first.

Having loved like this, how does anybody stay unhurt? No matter what you do, once you recognize and name it "love," there is damage.

Is the water getting higher? Am I closer to the ceiling?

And I remember the order of things. Things follow chronologically. There is order. Time moves forward. Creatures are born. And then they die. And then they live. No. They die last. Dying is the last thing we do. We absolutely do not remember seeing our mothers being born. There is order. One, two, three, four, five, seventy, forty-two, ten, 2,319, twenty-two, 10,098, thirteen…what? There has to be order. The number five is followed by…ummm…three, four, five…Four, and then Five, and then…What's wrong with me?

A sharp inhalation.

I remember dying. I remember when I died. I have the fragmented details of my own death. I know my last breath. I remember it. How can that be?

And then there is the sound of moving water. Somewhere in her cave, the water is beginning to move.

"The meeting of two personalities is like the contact of two chemical substances. If there is any reaction, both are transformed."

—Carl Gustav Jung

one

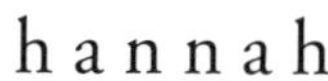

hannah

Imagine a love between two people that demands space in your consciousness. If you move too close, you become gently aware of a silent latitude. But this thing cannot be placed in space. It has no soft longitude. No mass. Yet it elbows you in the ribs as it pushes by. You step back. Small confused steps. You attempt to see what it was that just touched you. But your eyes find nothing.

Or suppose you are standing on the shore of a lake and suddenly, out of the calm, moon-less night, there are waves. Perhaps a boat is pushing through the water out there, in the middle. Listen. You don't hear anything. Wait. The shushing sound of waves pushing against the shore fills your ears. The effect of some *thing* has reached you. Can you guess the story of the thing out there by looking at the almost regular arriving of waves? These waves are trying to tell you something. Will listening to them give you the story? Would it help if you took your shoes and socks off and waded into the icy, black water? You are standing at the edge of the lake with evidence of some story in front of you. That's all you have to go by.

Do you need this story fixed in place and time? Is that what you're used to? Does it really matter where this story takes place? A city? A town? An ocean liner? A bedroom? Or perhaps you're imagining this. You do have a very active imagination. And your memory, well, there are adjustments to be made as time passes. Is memory something we still have, or is it something we've lost?

Love is love, you might believe. Place and time are unimportant when it comes to love. But the land is very important to this story. Whether it's for the sake of metaphor, or flavour, or the sense of vastness or closeness, the land plays a role. And time, well, time is a little mixed up. Oh, it's not science fiction if that's what you're thinking. It's love. And it's a misaligned memory. But mostly, it's love.

In this story, the land is always in the corner of your eye. It vies for your attention. The landscape steals from the cerebral. You are in the mountains. Here is a landscape worthy of an intricate love. Mountains are a landscape where a huge love could almost pass unnoticed. It would have to be quite extraordinary to catch your attention. You could be looking up at that glacier, all elephantine and vast, and right behind you: Tristan and Isolde, or Romeo and Juliet. And you would suddenly feel rather odd. Is that your lunch? you might think. Maybe you've eaten something that's off. Maybe you're getting the flu. What the hell is that?

The mountains, for you, are a very large distraction from anything worldly. When you come towards the peaks there is a leaving behind of worries. They drop in the wake of your car like a swirl of new snow. Perhaps, in the fall, you always go backpacking. One last kick at it before winter. Backpacking is something you do quite a bit. So you park your car near the trail-head, trudge along beside the highway under the burden of your pack. Then you become stolen by the dense pines. You climb up through the degrees of the trail blind to any view except the trunks of trees. Finally, across a small, marshy opening, you are shocked by the closeness of Mount Fitzwilliam. The sky is cut in half by your proximity to the mountain. She's almost hanging over top of you, all thrust up and out.

You're alone, high up in the Fitzwilliam Basin, on the edge of Jasper National Park. You're camped at the edge of a lake. When you wake up it's too quiet. Something feels wrong. As you crawl out of your tent to perform your morning ablutions you notice the mountains are softly upside-down on the surface of the lake. It's cold, almost before sunrise and everything is silver. There in a corner of the lake, two geese peel themselves from the barely-mirrored water as if in an other, slower time.

There. That's all you need to start. Geese mate for life. That's what they say. For life. You begin to remember Hannah.

You remember the meadows across from Mount Edith Cavell. When the two of you stopped working the legs, rested for just for a minute, your heat was peeled away so quickly. With the first steady charge of cold off that mountain, you both began to freeze. Even the comforting hiss of the gas stove offered little solace.

In that brown spring meadow, your hands curved blue tin cups of hot Earl Grey tea, then quickly numbed again once the tea was gone. And all around you, the life hadn't begun to stir. Grasses sighed in cool wind. Edge waters barely transformed from icy razors to minuscule trickling water, and alpine flowers only dreamed of poking up in their impossible places. Cavell was an immense, uncaring wall of granite. High up near the summit there was still snow scarring her face. The snow up there persisted through the day while everything down here was hopeful.

And look across the valley at this lumbering glacier you've suddenly discovered. Do you get the feeling it cares about you, or Hannah, or about time. It slugs forward, or draws backward, with prodding from gargantuan periods of warming or freezing climates. This glacier grinds away at the earth and rock regardless of whether its movement is forward or backward. Here is the creation of new valleys of fertile land, you think. Glaciers are very old stories. They do not care about anything small. With thousands of years to ponder, glaciers make time irrelevant. And in the looming shadow of a glacier, love is an almost imperceptible scratch on a slab of granite.

⊱⊰

You're looking awfully hard at this. How can you see the beauty when you look so closely at something? Look at the edges. Prevaricate. Look at the jagged edges where it's ripped. There's the beauty.

Oh, you don't recall where you were when she said: "There's so little time left. I can feel it ticking away, and it weighs on me. Doesn't it bother you?"

What did she mean saying that? Were you dying? Was there an asteroid heading towards Earth? Or had she decided to go east, across the country with her husband and their children? Was she leaving that lovely thing you stumbled into, to be with him, to raise her children like a good mother, a good wife? And will she create a sort-of stalemate between she and her husband? Will she be happy? Phone her up and ask her. She'll make a metaphor that will cause your head to spin. You'll think you got an answer to your question but really all you have are ten more questions. And now, there is a time difference between this world, your world, and hers. Now, she is always three hours ahead of you. She rises three hours before you do. Sleeps three hours before you.

⊱⊰

It was as if you were waking bears, stunned with hibernation. You found each other and before looking to food, you began to love. You began to pant with desire.

Look around. Find the edges. Time means nothing to this rock, these grasses, this brilliant moss, or this rarefied view. And the seasons? They just move.

But this morning, in your Fitzwilliam basin, alone and cold in that soft light, you doubt if anything you experienced with Hannah could be viewed as a segment of time. None of your experiences with her can be named. You two don't belong in time. Hours, months, days, decades, minutes. All these things seem silly now.

But you can close your eyes, and live the two of you tangled in the dreamy fallout of love-making. Hands lulling each other in the dark, smoothing skin, a focused remembering of the smallest details of skin. And outside it is raining. A dog barks three times, then four, then two more. A car shushes by the house. There's a branch from the poplar out front scratching the window pane in the wind. A heady rain scent fills the room.

Do you remember Hannah lying on the floor of your apartment, on her back, surrendered to the Bach violins, seeking an early escape. And then fragile alpine grasses, flowers covered the bed. And pine scent flowed carefully across cool sheets. You two created a quiet place where mattering things could easily be destroyed. Here was a religion of distraction, a philosophy of *dangerous* temporality. You understood the ending but did not attempt to rationalize toward anything noble. Part of this was so common that it disgusted you.

The end was there in each moment. Your beginnings were embedded in each whisper. The end always takes care of itself. Independent and constant, the end was nothing to concern yourselves with.

Perhaps at the end of this chapter, you will be remembered accurately by someone you do not know.

Oh, you're confused. Did you expect to remember this in order? Does memory work that way? Or do odd things we stumble upon spasm us into memory? A scent. A quality of light. A taste. A word. Three words. You're trying to not look directly at something in exactly the wrong order.

At the beginning of your story, near the beginning anyway, you already know about your visit to Mount Edith Cavell in the spring. "Glaciers," she'll say, standing looking at one, "all remind me of gushing vaginas."

"Such a warm image on top of something so cold," you say. You try to make your voice light. This isn't a criticism, it's only observation.

Did she hear you? Or did the wind take your words and throw them behind those rocks. Perhaps a pica or a marmot hears you but Hannah doesn't.

The mountains are perfect for you. Insane love can march with impunity amongst so much rock and pine and narrow sky. You belong there. And you know you will stand in the first few paragraphs of this story waist deep in aliveness and turn away from two lifting geese in the pre-dawn.

When you first discovered each other, you were drunk. If you were sober, you would probably have understood the horrible timing. You might have steered away from your about-to-happen adventure but that's unlikely. Hannah pushed you into the trunk of your car with a kiss as you tried to unload her bike. You abandoned the car for a taxi. You searched for condoms in the middle of the night. Drank cheap scotch with mountain spring water. And you fell in love with her inside her first tenderness toward you. Something as simple as her hand on your back. Her caressing you gently into place. And later, her scent, all her smells. The curve of her armpit against striped sheets. Hannah sprawled across the bed. Her hip bones rising. The small slope of pubic mound; a soft scree-slope. Hannah, lying across the bed.

She will get to walk across the street to the bus station in the spring rain. At the very end, she will get the sweet, romantic finale. You will sit stupidly in your car. And you will not wait. Oh no, not you. Instead of waiting to see if she turns her head, you will drive away. Observers might think she is going away for the weekend, to visit her sister or her mother. They will never imagine what it really is. And if she'd turned, in the middle of the street? What would you have done? If she had turned and dropped her bags on the road, with tears streaming down her face, and the rain everywhere hazily descending? What?

Would have. Could have. Should have. Fuck it. You stand shivering, inside the beginning scenes of a narrative, as the two geese fold themselves into a disarranged blackness, lose themselves over the pointed beginnings of detail across the lake. And at some point in your story, after you've left her in the mountains perhaps, a numbness; a cold, dark lake on the way home to the city. And nothing but metal comfort. She wanted a last day by herself. "I'll take a bus home tomorrow," she says. You'll stand there and remember everything that has happened. Inside a heart beat, you will remember and then a shiver along your spine. Memory is all you have. No pictures, no drawings or sketches. Only memory.

If only you'd met her before. Is that what you think? That by some miracle, if you'd met her before her husband came along you and Hannah would be together and happy? But she would not be the same Hannah. You would not be the same person you are. You might be her husband. Another character might be playing your role. You cannot decide whether what you had was real or not.

And all around you during your story, are mountains. You know many ways to draw a picture of a mountain. You sketch them whenever you stop during your hikes. And you know how to sustain the mystery of a thing while describing it. You look at its outline. You've always know this to be true. Well, it's a theory of yours. How does the mountain mass up against the sky? Where is the jagged line of the horizon? How do pines force veins of green up slopes. When it rains, what do you smell? What do you feel? What do the clouds taste like?

If you look at the peripheries of things, you are thinking, the mystery, the magic, can remain. So you look back with only fleeting glances. A snippet here, a sharp detail there. You do not want the mystery of what you had to disappear. You do not want the half-life of a memory. You do not want these fragmented memories of actual events being replaced by what you wish to remember. In the end, we are often left with a lie of our own devious manufacture. And the memory? The memory becomes something other than a clear reflection of that reality.

⊱⊰

It was almost two years ago, at Cafe Select, on 106th Street. Remember? She sits across from you in that dark restaurant and announces she has left her husband. How can it be that it means nothing to you? You only think that it's sad. You do not think about the opportunity. But you already love her. You've loved her from the first time you talked with her in a gallery on the South side. You loved her for her soft, French accent and firm opinions about art. And you loved her because you did not understand her sculptures. You don't even think for a moment about her husband and what he might be going through.

"I'm sorry," you say to her. "Are you okay?"

⊱⊰

Hannah begins to smoke and drink too much in her life.

⊱⊰

You've been drinking wine before you find the loon. You were in a restaurant in Calgary, on 16th Street, drinking red wine. The loon is damaged and as she cradles it in her arms, you see fear in her eyes. You find the bird during one of your excursions in a Calgary park. You decide you cannot kill it to save it from suffering. It does not seem to be in pain. Frightened and vulnerable, somehow, the loon allows Hannah to pick it up. Perhaps Hannah fears the black and white world. It is not that she prefers gray but it seems that imprecision is her road. She attempts to live in the now of this pleasure but for her it is difficult. She's told you that she has already made the hard choices. You can imagine that sometimes the thought of her children and her husband seem too immense a cargo to push aside.

⊱⊰

You pull your camera from your pack. You want to capture her here in this meadow. Sunlight peering over Cavell's massing shoulder lights her hair on fire as she looks back at you. You realize how beautifully at home Hannah is here. Something shines from her in these mountains. You raise your camera. Hesitate. Then lower it. Make the decision to remember.

⁂

If you had raised your camera on this same day, four years ago, you would have seen the beginning movements of a climb across the valley. If you'd been there in the meadow, you'd have seen a group of climbers move silently through the parking lot in the early morning. Ghost shadows moving up towards you. Three of them have headlamps. The beams swing through the dark in broad swatches.

They have about 2,000 metres of climbing in front of them. Cavell is 3,363 metres, just over 11,000 feet. One of the climbers slogging up towards the meadow is thinking about death, but it's not a serious contemplation. He would not want to climb with people he'd be repulsed to die with. Bob is happy with the climbers he's pulled together for this climb. A talented group with temerity tempered. It's Bob who thinks of mountains in feet. It's his philosophy that mountains seem more friendly when measured that way. Metres don't make sense to him. Feet just seem easier to understand. People too. It's hard to visualize someone as being 188 centimetres tall. Easier to comprehend "six-foot-two." Instead of 188 small things, it was six mid-sized things and a couple of small ones. Easier to see in your mind.

The night before, they had walked down from the road from the hostel to scout the trail that lead to the base of the primary ridge. They'd heard it was easy to get lost in the bony fingers of moraine and sure enough, it was difficult to see the route. They were dwarfed by Angel Glacier at sunset, with Cavell hovering above.

Someone in the group of climbers is thinking the glacier looks like a frozen Jesus on the cross, his feet in the small blue lake, veined arms along the upper ridge.

And one of the climbers is excited beyond belief to actually be back climbing after a long winter of working out on indoor climbing walls.

One of the women has to pee.

Michelle is thinking about her left boot. There's a pinch along the top of her foot. Tomorrow, she'll try a different way of tying. Maybe a thinner pair of socks.

They bring their tea with them, in tin camp cups. The wind has been ruined, relinquished to a hush. A sequestered calm defends the valley. Someone has a bottle of cognac. "Best to keep any rope in our packs tomorrow," Bob says. "But there is new snow up there. It's always good to have rope." He is, for the most part, talking to himself in the pensive company of climbing companions.

The next morning, they turn off their headlamps as the sun rises. Six of them stand at the base of the ridge, adjust packs, joke about how much goddamned rope they have. It's not a difficult climb. The East Ridge is rated a three out of six for over-all difficulty. And the most difficult technical climbing a five-point-three on a scale of five-point-zero to five-point-ten. Although, Bob had seen a five-point-eleven in Dougherty's *Selected Alpine Climbs.* It's more a scramble than a climb for an experienced climber. Regardless of this fact, they are all equipped with crampons and ice axes. They would have to go through unavoidable snow and ice near the summit.

If you'd been there four years ago, you would have seen the party of climbers move toward the first ridge. You would have watched for as long as you could see them. Then when dawn moved into the valley, stingy with pink light, you'd have first heard, then seen, a single crow at the top of a pine tree. The crow, scratching the silence with its caws appears to be grumpy, you might have thought. A single crow. One for sorrow, two for joy. You might have looked around for a second or a third crow.

But you were not there. Four years ago you were walking around the streets of Paris, on a working vacation. Trying in vain to resurrect your high-school French. You were lonely in Paris. You were writing mooshy love letters to a woman in Edmonton—spilling your heart. And when you arrived home, she was not there at the airport to pick you up. She'd promised to be there but she was not. She phoned you a week later and said she was sorry and that was it. She prescribed a good single malt scotch for the pain, as if she was worth suffering over while stoned on something expensive. You clearly remember looking around at the crowd, not seeing her face, seeing other people hugging and kissing. And the sinking feeling in your gut. Looking back, you realize you were probably just very, very lonely. The writer Kurt Vonnegut Jr. (he dropped the Jr. part as he grew older) said loneliness is the number one affliction facing mankind. Not heart disease, not cancer. Loneliness. In fact, in his novel *Slapstick; or, Lonesome No More!* he proposes a system for providing every person in America with a vast extended family.

You were not there to watch the beginning moves of this climb. These climbers form a story at the edge of your focus. They define your story by sitting carefully at its edge, further back in time. You are in love with the idea of looking at the edges of things.

Up in that meadow, you suddenly want it all to clash. You want a noisome helicopter to land here, now, and spit forth tourists with video cameras, loud and awful, fat and ugly. Tourists who have not done the work with their legs to arrive at this place. Tourists who do not care about the peace or dignity of this place. Tourists who would look around and say "My God, Martha, what the hell happened to summer? It's too cold up here!" or "This would be a good place for a hotel, huh?" or children screaming "We want to watch TV!" Only they could crash this dream and turn it nightmare.

And you do not want this life to clash. You do not want this passing image. You already possess scratched-in-rock memories of this just-happening life. All those repulsive ideas do not belong here. The only pain you'll have to face is hidden. You're an innocent in this area. When she leaves. That's when you'll find out.

And what will you do without her smoothing hand? Will you fold yourself into this clear reality, watch leaves…ochre, rune, quiet yellow, burnt orange, earth brown, fire red? See them drop to pattern the ground, feel the waltz of new snow in the wind, smell the too-green summer push its own furthest boundary?

You will let this end all right. But after, after this strange dream in cool wind and uncaring shadow of Cavell, with images of her wedged against frosted granite, and silver, scraping glacier.

You don't even remember where you were when you said: "I don't think of you in terms of days. I can't think like that. Minutes don't apply. Not while I'm with you. I don't want hours and minutes or weeks. I'm living whatever comes, whatever makes sense." You look at her and realize she is intensely listening. "Or in your case," you add, "whatever doesn't make sense. Whatever's blissful, insane, painful and, and joyful."

She says nothing but rolls on top of you. With her hand she guides you between her legs. And her eyes do not waiver from yours. Everything exists there. At the outer edge of her eye there is a clarity of blue you've not seen before. Perhaps the colour of Gentians in the rain. You lean into the cool breeze off Cavell. You can feel the stones of her weight press into your back. She arches into an icy breeze. Her image is frozen: soft, sloping breasts juxtapose Cavell's hard, fractured face.

But nothing lasts here. The growing season is only a few months. It's a mirage of pleasure; temporary, fragile, and ultimately very short.

She is ripping from you. You were always ripping from each other. And below, a melancholy licking of waves brushes against this morning shoreline.

Peripheries. You are thinking about peripheries. Who is at the edge of your story?

Perhaps there is a woman from the town of Jasper, named Frannie, who works two jobs as waitress in order to stay living in the mountains. She walks along the shore of a lake with her dog. It's overcast and dark. There's a cool green smell. She wears a beret and tan-colored leather gloves, expects to see her breath but does not.

"Here, Pal," she says, and throws a drift-stick not too far out.

The dog scampers to the lake shore. There are still chunks of ice floating like confused sheep at the edges of the lake. Pal will not go in. The dog looks at her, looks at the bobbing stick, looks up at her, barks staccato into dark blue, but does not go into the water.

"That's okay," she says to the retriever, "I wouldn't go in tonight either."

Frannie ruffles Pal's head and neck. She adjusts her beret and quickens her pace towards home.

⊱—o—⊰

There is no toilet in this room. A sink only. Hannah silhouettes against a screened window. Naked, she is painted soft and ragged-edged by the diffused light. Mountains behind her, pine green, the colour between purple and blue stretched thin. One foot up on the sink counter, water rushing, Hannah washes. She washes you from her crotch. Her back is to you. This washing, a final element of your love-making.

You do not know what to think, stand by the door and watch, fascinated by this scene. Her curves against the pines. The brown of her skin meshed with green and blue. Here is an image that you will want to hold too tightly.

You're in a small hotel room in Jasper, in the Rocky Mountains. All the decisions have been made. It's just timing now. Hannah will go back to the east, figure out how to parent the best she can. And you will not wait for her resolutions. You will not wait to see what comes out. You will leave her here, in the mountains, drive back to the city and what will be, will be. You have always been at the edge of her life and that's where you will remain.

⊱—o—⊰

"You won't write," you say. "It doesn't matter."

"I'll write when I can."

"And no good-bye scenes," you say. "Promise me, no backward glances."

"I'll write when I can," she says.

"You've been well loved," you say and immediately regret sounding ridiculous, sentimental, dull, stupid.

She pulls at your hip, moves you closer. "You are well loved, my darling. I'll write you when I can," she says, her voice a tiny, resigned thing.

She's asleep when you wake. There's a thick sex smell in the small room. The sweet aroma pleases you. You pull cold water to your face and dress quietly. Downstairs in the bar of the hotel, sitting calmly on the floor, is a golden retriever. It looks up sleepily as you come in.

"Could I get a scotch and soda please," you say to the waitress.

"Any scotch do ya?" she says smiling across the bar at you.

"Any scotch will do me."

She slows down and really looks at you. Captures you with an intense stare that won't release. Creates an awkward silence.

"You all right?" She pours golden liquid into a glass.

"Nice lookin' dog. Yours?" You pause, offer a small smile.

"Yes, well, it's more like I'm hers." She glances at the glass. "I'm not being nosy or anything and you can tell me to go to hell if you want, but you seem kinda down."

"I'm fine." You sip your drink and smile quizzically. "You used good scotch?"

"Is it all right?"

"It's great. I just didn't expect a single malt scotch in a…"

"…dump like this?" she smiles.

"Well, I was going to say, a bar like this. An unexpected surprise. Thank you."

"My pleasure."

She's a tall brunette, her hair haphazardly pulled back into a loose ponytail. Several strands of hair fall across her face but she doesn't seem to mind. She wears a large, straw-coloured wool sweater with an elbow patch on the left arm. Dull ashen half-circles sit under her eyes. She looks beautifully fatigued, devastatingly weary. And then she destroys any image of exhaustion with a smile that is warm and comforting.

"Another beer, Roy?" she says to an elderly man in the corner booth who just nods.

"I thought it was illegal to have animals inside bars," you say.

"It is illegal," she says flatly and then yanks hard on the fridge handle causing a suction sound.

"Oh." You pull something of yourself back.

She pours another scotch and soda, places it in front of you.

"I didn't order a…"

"…you just look like you could use it. It's on me." A shiver runs through her. She folds her arms across her chest.

Perhaps she's feeling the awkwardness of this. Something doesn't feel right here. She looks uncomfortable. It's as if every interaction between you is forced into place, contorted.

You finish your drink, leave the bar, walk up creaky, carpeted stairs. You can imagine her sitting there looking vacantly into the space where you just were.

And then, in the corner, Frannie will sit down with Roy.

"We're all broken," Roy will say. "We all need fixing."

Frannie might rub the loose skin back of the dog's neck as Roy talks. That odd statement is probably one of the longest strings of words she's ever heard from him.

You imagine Roy as one of Jasper's few remaining veterans.

"Broken," he'll say again. Then a new reel of film will slip in between his eyes and the world. He'll sip his beer and not speak again.

"It was bloody cold last night," the man in the fur coat says. "What a damned country."

He stomps into the bar with a disdainful arrogance that makes Frannie dislike him almost immediately. What did he expect?

"Well, it's the mountains and it's early spring," Frannie says. "It stays cold here in the spring. Now what can I get ya?"

"Gin, neat," he says and sits down.

"Comin' right up."

"Took a helicopter up into the back country yesterday," he says. "Me and Mary. We damned near froze our asses off. Back home, the flowers are blooming already."

Frannie wants to let Pal fetch the man by his asinine neck. But Pal seems to like this guy. The dog walks over with a disinterested ennui, sniffs his leg and then curls up at his feet. Something about this bugs Frannie. This is her dog.

Later, she will think about a poet she heard in Edmonton last fall. She'll be caught in a dream, wondering what the hell this poet could have been thinking about when he said the mountains held pain. There is no pain in the mountains. There is no joy. The mountains don't care about pain or joy or the daft poet who suggested this possibility. People bring the pain and happiness, agony, bliss. They bring it here inside themselves.

What are you taking back to the city? You stop the car. This leaving is too smooth, you think. You want to section it. You wish for segments of leaving. You don't want this steady asphalt stream. At Talbot Lake, still within the mountains, you pull over to the edge of the highway. There are waves lapping down there somewhere. The shore line is obscured but it's all just degrees of blackness anyway. It's bone cold. You sense something immense. Absence of detail magnifies that feeling to proportions that nurture fear. Leaning against the car is a smooth comfort. There are details of warmth and speed and velocity with this car. This barren place aches. A semi-truck vibrates by and then, a cold after-chill. You can hear the quiet coming behind the truck, and inside that absence of sound is where she reverberates.

She said she loved to read a trashy novel sometimes. Occasionally she would zip through books which consisted of plot, plot and more plot. A shallow journey from A to B. And then B to C. And then C to D. Here, on the dark shore of Talbot lake, you are caught in an eddy between R and S. Returning and staying. Risk and safety.

Nick owns the Chickadee restaurant, underneath Tekarra Lodge on the outskirts of Jasper. He remembers her, you. You were here at his restaurant together, after hiking. Deliriously happy. Nick remembers the joy surrounding you better than Hannah does tonight. He watched as you laughed, drank scotch and wine, ate the pepper steak. He remembers yours was rare, hers, medium rare. Nick made the Greek coffee for you. In his memory, you were like children. You took your wine outside. Sat on the front verandah until two in the morning, laughing, drinking, in the mountain night.

"Nothing exists in a vacuum, right?" Hannah is looking up into a full, swarming bed of stars.

"Okay," you say.

"The Universe is a vacuum, right?" Her voice all strained, stretched by her upward gaze.

"Yes."

"And fire needs oxygen to exist, right?"

"Yup."

"Well, then explain the stars."

You have to think about that one. You've had too much wine to actually come up with anything resembling science. You look over at her and see she is smiling in victory.

"They're beautiful," you say.

In the dim light you can see her nod and close her eyes.

You insisted Nick join you. Together, you drank to many things. To life, to art and music, to chickadees and pine trees, the hummingbirds, and the stars. The stars that swarmed like a trillion iridescent bees.

That was the night you looked at Hannah and dreamed a life you had yet to experience. You dreamed Hannah across from you at a restaurant, breastfeeding your child. And she wouldn't miss a beat. She would pull aside her top, let the baby find the nipple and wouldn't stop her train of thought.

That night, it seemed you were there. The dream scene became real. It became true. This was your child, yours and

Hannah's kid. You imagined a profoundly level relationship. You imagined you were happier than you've ever been.

Sure, it was probably the wine, and being in the mountains, and sitting on the verandah, the indigo sky, Nick's good company…all of it. But for a few minutes you were lost in a blissful dream.

But Hannah already had children.

Perhaps Hannah's memory of this night hesitates. It's forced, elbowed against unmoving rock. It loses itself in eddies of wanting emotion. She desires the comfort of the memory but not the new stabbing sensation triggered by the same memory.

Nick looks long at her, from behind the bar. They held hands across table eight that night, he thinks. Something is injured here now. He takes her a glass of scotch with soda on the side. He says nothing. Places it in front of her with a quiet grace. There was no need to say anything. She smiles after he has already retreated from the table.

After the meal, her waiter asks if she is aware that she is crying.

"Yes, no, I don't know. Thank you," she says.

Nick brings her another glass of scotch, leaves her in peace. She sips her drink, looks out the window, drifts her vision out into the night. Later she writes in a notebook. Scribbles of feeling. Spastic curves and crosses. Encrypted visions and strings of sentences only she can decipher with any semblance of ease.

She remembers sitting across from you in a restaurant in Calgary. You wanted to know what it was that she'd written in her letter. You'd underlined garbled words, sentence fragments. You really wanted a translation.

Nick places other customers away from Hannah, watches over her. He thinks he knows what happened. Yes, there are details he can't know but he comprehends the story by the smell of sadness. The air seems bruised around her. She will get privacy while she is here, he thinks. This, I can assure. It's the least I can do.

Behind the hotel, Frannie watches sure and gentle clouds mass up at the western edge of town. They pillow each other gray against Mount Pyramid, begin to hold the town. She's thinking about all the men. When she first got to this town, its immediacy, and its transient nature was a strong aphrodisiac. Frannie bedded a lot of guys. But what the hell, she thinks. It was the eighties and for the most part, all you had to think about was something venereal or making a baby. A venereal disease was not a death sentence. Then there was Bob, a marriage, and happiness for a while. They kept delaying the idea of having children. They both wanted very much to have children but there were mountains to climb. And a lot of hiking and skiing to do. And there was money to save.

Then there was the accident. A stupid mistake. Three of the six climbers died. Bob and two others. It wasn't a difficult climb. That's the tragedy. They weren't up there reinventing the wheel.

She looks up at the high, ripped horizon. The clouds are thick and heavy with all the shades of gray and scattered blue.

She nods. There's snow coming.

"Come on, Pal," she calls.

The dog lopes up the alley towards her and they go back inside the bar.

After your first awkward loving at your apartment you came to the mountains with a different woman. Why would you do that? Because you'd already made this plan with Victoria, before Hannah. Before your world exploded. You came to the mountains with Victoria but your reeling and stunned compulsion was for Hannah. You did not know if you'd ever see Hannah again but could not shake the smell of her, the touch of her, the timbre of her voice. She lived in your gut. You were like an addict, desperate to numb an insane need. Her hands had shaped you into something wonderful, something you loved. You were suspended by desire. Every molecule of your being was screaming AGAIN! MORE! And you could not find a way to get what you felt out in the open. That is what you had to do. You were claustrophobic inside your own skin, and it was not going well with Victoria, who knew nothing of this other confluence. You and Victoria were staying at the Chateau Lake Louise. You were in trouble.

Later, you would begin to write poems. You try working out your feelings in short stories but the words weigh on you. The sentences oppress. You try writing letters but nothing you write quite manages to empty out your heart. You try to paint your heart with a small water-colour set, with no relief. You sit at the piano in your apartment and can not make the appropriate combinations of sounds to capture the joyful melancholy you feel.

You need the soul-cleansing work of a brilliant piece of music. The kind of music which gives your mood no place to go but into the music. But you do not find that music. You begin to write poems. Agonizing, pathetic, self-absorbed poems about what you're feeling. But you did not have an outlet for your feelings when you were at Lake Louise. Your feelings of need dizzied your heart, tortured you with illogical desire. And always, the persistent damn-the-consequences passion.

Even in the hot tub, surrounded by the peaks, you can only think of Hannah. Her hand on your back.

You drink far too much tonight. You get out of bed and sit stunned in semi-darkness.

"I'm just going to go out for a little walk," you say.

Victoria opens her eyes, looks at her watch. "It's 2 am for Christ's sake."

"I need air."

"That's what windows are f..."

On the ice there is dim moonlight. It is a long and deep lake. A spring sun has melted most of the snow and what remains is frozen, crunches under foot.

You imagine you are walking on your own skin. Translucent, dark veins track beneath the surface. Fifty metres out, past the warning signs a sharp, deep bang stops you. It comes from the bottom. Somewhere, there is a massive crack. You smile. Imagine sinking into this lake. Think: because you have made love with her, you are apparently reckless with your life.

Listen. Nothing. A distant train. Nothing. You see the drifting, sinking line of your body in the dark water.

The moon leans, offers scarcely enough light to get you to the end of this icy epidermis. You feel no choice. You can see the end of the lake. There. But could not guess how far it is. How long have you been walking? Distance is wrong, distorted. You could arrive at the flood plain in twenty steps, a hundred metres, two kilometres.

Evenly, you just walk. And going through this ice does not matter. You've decided there will be no fight, just a drifting and breathing of liquid cold into lungs, and no fight.

Victoria is asleep when you get back. You slump in an armchair and watch her. Wonder, what the hell are you doing here? This is so unfair to her. Sip scotch from a hotel bathroom glass. Appreciate the ribbed comfort of the glass in your hand.

In the morning it's raining, slowly disintegrating the snow. The weather is almost coastal. It's socked into the valley and a clear pine scent sticks in the air. The clouds suffer at the far end of the lake, sullen and irritable, they cut mountains in half.

You're civil and kind to Victoria at breakfast because you know you will see Hannah again. You know it is only the beginning of your story. You have to see her again. And she will try to not let it continue. The two of you will meet and agree to stop it. But you'll not be able to stop. You'll need to push it to the end.

Outside it is snowing heavily. It's drifting down and making a soft white blanket of the landscape. Frannie is alone in the bar, sitting calmly, looking outside. Pal rests at her feet under the table. It's two in the afternoon and it's begun.

Every month, all year 'round, she thinks. How anything grows here is beyond me.

Roy will arrive in twenty minutes for his regular beer. He will stomp his feet at the doorway and say "Frannie?" and she will know to deliver a beer to his table. The bastard American will come down to get away from the wife and he will probably complain about something out of his control.

Later, Roy will smile and nod and say this snow is to be expected.

Pal will act as though she has never seen it before.

And Frannie? She's tired. Fourteen-hour days prey on the body and the mind, and the narrow land in between. She sips her coffee. Scattered thoughts drift through her.

It doesn't smell like a bar in here today. Do I have enough beer for the weekend? What's keeping Roy? I wonder what this snow looks like disappearing into my lake? I wonder if that guy who knew his scotch is all right. He seemed in trouble. Like he was about to do something horrible.

She thinks about Bob. She thinks about him every single day of her life. He used to say it would be best to die doing something you love. Don't want to be curled up in a nursing home without my brain and without my memory, he'd say. Don't want the tubes and whimpering with food dribbling down my face.

We should be careful what we wish for, she thinks.

You think about Hannah. About how it might be possible to cozy up to clichés so repugnant to your senses that you'll wonder about your sanity. You'll both wonder about love. Perhaps in a few years, you'll meet in Toronto, far from the mountains, at a neutral cafe.

You'll order a bottle of Merlot. Drink it quickly out of nervousness. Not touch. Not talk about her family. Not discuss your romantic failings with other women. You will not talk about the weather. Perhaps, you have a conversation about the new Woody Allen film. The new piece she's working on. And then silence.

"When did romantic love become such a cliché," she'll say. "When did that happen? When did it begin to lose its power?"

"When we began to dissect it, to disseminate it," you'll say. "We look too closely. We think too much"

"But it's not hopeless. I feel…"

"…I can't erase the messages you left on my answering machine. I know that sounds pathetic but I can't. I listen to them again and again. I listen to your voice and it thrills me. I love your voice. I know I'm being pathetic. It disturbs me that I'm pathetic but…"

"…No. You're not pathetic. Never pathetic."

She'll touch your hand across the table and everything will begin again.

two

...everything will begin again

Everything will begin again. Isn't that romantic. Well, it won't be that easy. This has been very much like a fairy tale. Fairy tales were absolutely grim before they got cleaned up. Blood and puss and evil ruled. Death, death and more death. Perhaps the good guys didn't always win. Somewhere along the line the stories got sanitized. And then Disney came along and cleaned them up some more, squished them into mediocre pabulum for the masses, got them ready to make money for the corporation. So this love affair becomes an unabridged fairy tale. Something in you was damaged by this meeting and it takes you a very long time to figure out what it was. You don't know about Hannah. You only know she holds you in a place inside of her. You also know there are demons in her to which you were not introduced. Those demons, you imagined, were only visible in very bright light. It seems you never saw Hannah in bright light. It was always dull, or cloudy, or dim when you met. At times it felt like the two of you, through some twist of nature, created the weather. *Film noir* comes to mind. Although it has yet to be determined exactly how damaged you are by this experience, while you were in it, you really had no choice. You were both sucked along by forces you didn't understand.

Light. You remember the lemon tinge of morning before sunrise, walking home to your apartment from Hannah's house. You walked along the river, entwined in bird song and the cool morning, happy because you had been touching her, kissing her, loving her. And she had allowed you to help when she needed it. The two of you packed up her house. Her husband was long gone. Already in the east working a new job. You did not discuss the details of what you were doing. It was simply something that needed to be done. It was necessary that the house be cleaned. There was no need to talk about why it was being cleaned. You'd started late and worked through the night, making pot after pot of coffee. Hannah had tried to make the coffee but somehow, even when you were there helping, her coffee was horrid.

You remember the one time you actually enjoyed a cup of her coffee. You'd flown to Vancouver to meet her for the opening of a show which featured three of her pieces. You stayed with her in a friend's house, a large two-story brick building. In the morning, a blue mug beside the bed, the smell of coffee, steam serpentining. Out the window, new snow high up on distant mountains, glorious gray sky. And music. Hannah was playing flamenco music. Fingers of guitar floated down the hallway, echoed perfectly through high-ceilinged rooms. This memory melts all the hardness out of you. You love this memory. You try not to think about how you felt the night before, or the night after. You try to look at it quickly, and then just as quickly look away. That morning you could imagine a lifetime of similar mornings. Here was a memory, which if you looked hard at, and thought about the fact that it was the only such morning, well, it could cause you pain. So you look away. You avoid blue coffee mugs. You make flamenco music a thing almost loved from a distance, like an ex-lover across the room at a party.

You are stunned with a tragic feeling of missed opportunity. You question yourself. Should you further interject your life into hers? Do you follow her out to the coast and continue with this affair? Do you leave your family, your friends, your work? Do you step into the oar-less boat and drift out into the sea with no food or water, only your faith? How much do you love this woman? There would be confrontation at the other end. And you hate confrontation. There is no way you wouldn't wind up in a room with the husband. Do you see what you just did? You objectified the husband. There! You did it again. His name is…shit, you can't remember his name. Call him *Norm* for now. You will probably wind up in a small room with Norm and you'll have to duke it out for this woman. Not fisticuffs. You'll probably want to just fire words back and forth. But Norm will likely not roll over like a good dog. Hannah is the mother of his children for Christ's sake. The guy might want to get violent. Do you love Hannah enough to get in a fistfight over her?

Not your style. You'd go out there and begin to seduce from a safe distance.

Then you start to think about your morality. You remember reading a Hemingway passage about morality. He wrote about being able to look yourself in the eye in the morning. And if you can do that, and like what you see, then you've been moral the night before. But you're no Hemingway. In fact, from what you've seen and read, Hemingway was no Hemingway.

Can you look at yourself in the mirror in the morning? Yes, of course you can. But you're not looking at yourself. You're looking at an image of how you feel when you are with Hannah. You're looking at your own desire. You're looking through a filter of dumb love.

Let her go, part of you screams. Don't contact her. Don't write her. Let her be. The other part of you recognizes how wonderful you felt being with her. It says, consider going out there. Listen to your heart. Follow your bliss. Your heart says do it. Take the risk. Tomorrow you could die. You were happy beyond belief with Hannah. Go after her.

Happy? What do you mean happy? You were hurting Norm. Every time you saw her, Norm was taking a hit. Oh, he didn't know every time but he knew enough. Hannah was living with a friend in an apartment downtown. She went home every day to take care of the kids. She slept in the apartment on nights she wasn't with you. Hannah, you find out later, was pretty open about what she was doing with you. She told Norm just about everything. Your mother used to say, you can't build your happiness on someone else's unhappiness. But your mother could not have understood the steamy world in which you were submerged.

By the time Hannah left, your relationship was at its critical mass. Passion had blown up into a storm of something uncontrollable. It folded over and hunched into something seemingly small, and then exploded again into a massive and even more frightening thing. You remember a storm from when you were young. You were perhaps thirteen or fouteen years old. In the mountains for a couple of weeks, you were staying with friends in a small cabin, in an old mining town. It was July. It was July and it began to snow in the center of the afternoon. A storm bulldozed its way through the narrow valley and dumped a thick wet whiteness. When it was done and the snow seemed to be tapering off, you remember the zinc colour of the sky, the heady humid scent, and the overwhelming, muffled silence. At twilight, the wind changed directions and blew the storm back up the valley. The storm dumped snow on the tiny village with a renewed steadiness. By morning there was over a foot of snow on the ground. You were trapped there for three days.

Zinc is probably one of those words you've seen used a few times; one of those words you think you understand but you're not quite sure. You appreciate the digression of looking something up in the middle of a narrative or following a path in the woods without a clue or a map. So you open the dictionary:

zinc: …2) a purplish gray that is lighter and slightly bluer than crane, bluer and paler than dove gray or granite, and bluer than cinder gray…

The colour *zinc* exists for you only in that sky. An after-snow sky is always the colour of *zinc.*

No backward glances. You'd talked about not looking back. What is the likelihood that you'll spend the rest of your life looking back? You made stupid promises to each other about never doing that. But you had no idea that you'd be driving her to the airport. You thought it was final when she drove across the country with a U-haul trailer. That would have made a good ending, a non-ending. You thought it was final when she got on a Greyhound bus in the spring. That was a good ending. It was uncluttered. But this prolonged loving. She stayed with you when she came back for the last time. She had a commitment at the university, a three-day course to teach. They were buying the airfare. Hannah, it seemed to you, was covering as many different means of travel in her leaving as possible. And so you tasted each other again, before the end. You were tempted to push it further than it was meant to be. Push it into something solid. And how would you do that? You have no idea. Perhaps by embracing the mundane. Perhaps by finding something grounded in reality.

But what if the Buddhists are right? This is all illusion. Life, the illusion of self, the illusion of existence, everything is completely transitory. You remember seeing a living, symbolic definition of the transitory nature of life in a ceremony where monks painstakingly used fine patterns of coloured sand to make an incredible work of art. It took them days of backbreaking work to make their mandala. At the end of that creative process was the acceptance that everything is transitory. They wiped it out. They destroyed the beauty they created.

You both ignore time. You know when she will leave yet you push it aside and let it be a last minute thing. Neither of you want to acknowledge the fact you likely won't see each other ever again. So you deal with simple things like skin and mouths and sweat. You drink a little more than usual. And perhaps there is a little more desperation in your loving. And then you are standing at the airport. You're in a line-up, waiting to check Hannah's bag. Velvet ropes between silver poles define your space.

"I don't know," you say.

She looks at your eyes. "Neither do I."

"I can't define, form…this." You look at her suitcase. A blue tag with numbers. A small rip in one corner of the suitcase.

"It's all right," she says softly.

You want to have begun leaving already. You want to be on the road back to Edmonton. You want to be three months from now. You want to be lying in your bed alone, tonight. And you want to hug her so hard that you leave an imprint of your love on her body. Perhaps you will both carry the fossilized remains of this love. Strangers will look at the wrinkles on your faces and say: Oh, I see. Yes, I understand.

"Impossible to step back from this and see how absurd it…"

"…always the writer," she says smiling.

"I'm just going to walk away."

"Good. That's best, I think."

"Yes, that would be best."

"Good then," she says.

"Yes. Good."

Run! Something in you says: RUN! Put it behind you already! Put her behind you! She's going home for Christ's sake! She's going home! How many times do you have to say good-bye? But you do not run. Instead you fall into her and hang on for several years. Then, after ten years. After you've lived together and had three children. After living on the west coast in a boat with two dogs and a cat, and after multitudes of lovemaking, and long, twisting conversations and too much theatre and too many ridiculous discussions about the nature of art. And after growing a little older together, and after experiencing the mundane mechanisms of daily existence. After finding out she sometimes talks in her sleep. After finding a lump in one of her breasts. After being angry at each other and making up. After all this—you finally let go. You turn around and walk through the doorway without another stupid word. And you do not look back. You wander through the parkade to your car, open the door, and curse the fact her scent is there. But even that will fade, you think. It'll all go in time.

Sometimes when you are pursuing a word in the dictionary, you'll wind up looking at a word on the same page you hadn't expected to find. Or perhaps on the page before. A word will demand attention. A *zephyr* for instance, is a mild gentle wind or breeze. Or a *zig*, an abrupt angled movement. You like the word *zig*. It seems your life is a long series of zigs. Well, zags too. You're having sharp changes in direction. But zephyr. Zephyr is a truly exotic yet practical word. A zephyr through the trees. A zephyr down the valley. Hannah was a zephyr in your life. Or at least she could be. Well, she could have been. Truthfully, she was a goddamned hurricane. But isn't zephyr a lovely word?

You revisit the nun. In your dream, Domonique is standing beside a dark car. Her back is touching cold metal and glass. Is the door unlocked? She doesn't know. Perhaps around the other side. Perhaps that door is unlocked? Does she have a key? No. The keys are in the ignition. Well then, one of the doors must be open. Domonique is looking across a broad meadow filled to overflowing with shrubs—willow and stunted poplar. The scene is frozen, held as a moment. Nothing moves. And then, as in all good dreams, something starts to happen. There is a rustling in the middle of the meadow and something begins to move towards her. But she cannot see what it is. There's something big causing the shrubs to move aside and Domonique instantly wants to run. But her legs won't move. Run! Run, you fool! But nothing works. And the thing is getting closer. If only she could turn around and get inside the car. She'd be safe there. She doesn't know if her door is unlocked. Her legs are locked and frozen and a panic moves up her body until she wants to scream but her voice too, is paralyzed. She can open her mouth but nothing—no sound. Now the thing is almost in the ditch. Soon she will see what it is. It's coming right for her. The bear rises up out of the ditch and drives towards Domonique. It's a fall bear, she thinks, fat and round, but also crazy with hunger for the impending hibernation. The bear is a steel blue colour. I'm going to die, she thinks. I'm going to be mauled. I'm going to die…but then the bear stops just short of her, its nose at her crotch. It sniffs, and veers around the front of the car and is soon across the road and gone into the trees. It brushes against her leg when it goes past. She does not feel it but she begins to imagine what the bear smell is like. Musty sweat, thick animal scent, and green—all the pine and grass, juniper, alpine flowers—everything this bear must have touched.

And then Domonique is in bed. She has been dreaming. It is her dream you have been eavesdropping on. She has the pillow strangled between her legs. It was so real, she's thinking. A window above the bed is wide open and there are sprinkles of snow sifting through, touching her face like a cold feather. Her shoulders are cold. She moves her legs, and her arms, just to make sure. She reaches a hand down to feel the calf of her left leg.

Was it your dream or this faceless nun's dream? Domonique's face is a mystery to you. You can't imagine what she looks like. But this is ridiculous. Surely you're not sharing dreams with a nun you've only conjured up out of a newspaper article you read months ago.

three

nigredo

It takes you three weeks to decide not to decide. However, you do make a pact with yourself to send her a poem a week for a year. You will not step into an oar-less boat and drift out to sea. You'll pace and fume on the beach, write poems, seal them in bottles and then toss them into the ebb and flow, the coming and going of waves. Something in you thinks this is romantic. And it probably is romantic. It's also a dangerous hook for both of you. At the end of this year you'll know. You're not a poet but poetry allows you to be insane. This is important because you feel insane with yearning. Poetry momentarily stops the yearning.

So, you would unabashedly send them to her. You would not tell her they were coming. You would not send letters. And then after a year, if you still had feelings, you could think about action. You would take a year and see where you stood in your heart. You would stand still, frozen with indecision like a big dumb Hamlet. You're either a coward, or you're noble, or you're just plain dumb. But one thing is certain. You had to be aware that each poem would be a hook. With each poem, there was the possibility that she would be hooked a little deeper, a little harder.

But what about her? What about Hannah? What if she's happy with it like this? What if everything you experienced was not the same for her? What if she's just not interested in staying connected? You only hope she feels the same way as you. You do not have anything resembling assuredness when it comes to Hannah's feelings for you.

Yet there was a moment when you knew for certain. You remember it clearly. You're in an Italian restaurant talking about a Wim Wenders film. Or was it Woody Allen's *Shadows and Fog?* No, it was Wenders' *Wings of Desire.*

"I love the way he allows for the slow unraveling of a narrative," she says. Then Hannah looks at you and says it in a whisper. She says it with a desperation, almost confused: "I want you." Her words fall out of the middle of your conversation. It is as if she has no choice but to acknowledge this simple fact and her realization has come in the middle of some other thought.

Now, this sounds stupid. We say we want things three hundred times a day. But when you heard her, you understood. She wanted you in her life. Even though that was likely not going to happen on a permanent basis, she wanted it to happen. It was an acquiescence to a misery that was about to occur. She wanted you! Read up on Tristan and Isolde. That was probably the first thing Isolde said after drinking that love potion. She probably said I want you, and felt an overwhelming feeling of love for this man who had killed her fiancé and was taking her away to marry a completely different man. Isolde probably had the same unbelievable, stunned look on her face.

Looking back, you could have stood up at that moment, gently kissed Hannah and walked out of her life forever. It was enough to be wanted that way. She wanted to share the mundane everyday life, and the extraordinary. She wanted to go there, with you. She wanted the whole package and that made you feel pretty damned good.

Just before Hannah left, something was about to happen. All things were possible but perhaps only a few options were plausible. You might solidify. Define edges. Step out of the imaginary land of affairs. Talk about the future, together. Risk seeing each other in the bright glaring sunlight. Risk making your desires visible to her. Risk rejection. She will always choose her children over you. That is how it should be.

Separation with no real resolution is another possibility. You say good-bye like good little troopers.

But you have been leaning into a heavenly wind at the edge of a cliff. You're leaning far out over the abyss. The wind is so strong and steady that it holds you up. You're able to lean far beyond the point of losing balance. You've been feeling very, very alive. And now, you only have a memory of that uncontrollable experience. It begins to haunt you as you try not to think about it.

Flat and simple destruction is also a possibility. You and Hannah fall apart just as quickly as you came together. You push into areas she's trying to avoid with her husband or her past. You start to become him. You stop being the escape from reality. And that ruins everything.

But it must go to shit in order for growth. The king is dead. Long live the king. Putrid mucky shitty decay is necessary. Out of ruin comes the potential for life, eventually.

An alchemist would likely say that everything is bitter—everything is rotten—in the beginning. The initial processes either lead to decay or have their beginning in rot. When Jung got going on alchemy and dreams, he said something like: in the *nigredo*, you feel like the whole world is falling apart and that this feeling itself will never go away. The future is in darkness and confusion. There is emptiness, isolation and everything is sluggish. Death is the only reality.

Perhaps you and Hannah were in the *nigredo* and didn't know it. Death of your time together was the only reality, a reality you consciously and repeatedly repressed. The weather was always gloomy. You often felt lost. Each moment was a new beginning. And if Jung's assertion that the *nigredo* is the initial phase of every single process in which transformation occurs, then what are you going to be at the end of this? What sort of butterfly will you be?

Passion, you find out by looking the word up, is a more complex notion than you imagined. Like most everyone you know, you understood it to mean sexual desire, or excitement about some thing.

Passion 1. strong emotion; outburst of anger (flew into a passion); sexual love; strong enthusiasm (for thing, for doing), object arousing this. **2.** the sufferings of Christ on the Cross (musical setting of) narrative of this from Gospels **3.** -flower, plant of genus Passiflora [flower of which was supposed to suggest instruments of the Crucifixion]

So, not just sexual desire. Jesus on the cross. The suffering of a martyr. That throws you for a loop. Passion? Jesus? Martyrs? You certainly didn't expect to find the word Jesus embedded in the definition of passion. You think you've been experiencing passion but Jesus hasn't really crossed your mind.

You wonder if passion is supposed to be a good thing. Because you've been thinking that if all the horrible suffering and pain Jesus went through is passion, then you'd rather pass. Was there joy for Jesus nailed to that tree? Was he happy to be taking the hit for all of mankind? A passional is a book of the sufferings of saints and martyrs. You're repulsed by the idea that you could be a martyr about anything. Maybe to love. But love doesn't care. This romantic love is like snow. It falls where it wants with a steady indifference.

You decide that "passion" isn't a very precise word. You'd like to find a good replacement.

People often accuse you of being a romantic. They often mean it as a negative thing. Romantics are flakes. They aren't grounded in reality and so on. In a world that defines "more" as better. And "bigger" as preferred. And "constant and prolific growth" as good. With all these givens, being a romantic is akin to being a loser. Hannah said you were romantic. But it was clear that she meant it as a positive quality. Are you? The fountain pen. When people get a glimpse of your fountain pen, it sometimes fosters a response about what a romantic you are. But many thousands of people in the world prefer fountain pens. Many of these people are likely *not* romantic. Perhaps, when you were young you always had a bottle of champagne and two glasses in the trunk of your car. "You just never know," you'd say.

Maybe you read *Zorba the Greek* at the right moment in your life.

Maybe you like to dance with strange women in Safeways while shopping for cheese.

Maybe you grew up thinking you weren't good for much, that you were not particularly attractive, that you were stupid. Perhaps you were so geeky as a child that you never quite made it into any group. You were always at the edge of things. This alleged charm; this romantic spirit grew out of a desperation for… love? Acceptance? Approval?

You certainly do not consider yourself romantic.

Romantic: 1. of characterized by, or suggestive of or given to romance, imaginative, emotional, remote from experience, visionary 2. (of music) subordinating from to theme, imaginative, passionate *3.* fantastic, unpractical, quixotic, dreamy 4. preferring grandeur or picturesqueness or passion or irregular beauty to finish and proportion, subordinating whole to parts or form to matter

You take out your pencil and scribble a number five in the margin: *5.* Someone who, even at a very, very old age, believes all things are possible.

⁂

April is a strange month. The embracing of a dichotomy. A movement from death to life. New life rises up through what has died. Tulips, close to the house, poke their red spike tongues through the dirt. You notice them this morning and think: *hmmm, life apparently goes on.*

You can't remember Hannah's face. You have no pictures of her. You've been thinking about your desire. You are sitting on the verandah of your apartment watching the Oilers play their first game of the playoffs on a little black and white television. You realize your affair with Hannah was unrealistic, ridiculous. The whole thing with you and Hannah had no palpable essence. The whole thing took place a foot off the ground. Any facts appearing in print will be lies. This whole story, if it were to be written, would be a grand lie. What is the truth of this story? Perhaps it's that romance demands a price. And often, we humans are willing to pay it, with zeal.

The telephone rings. You slide the screen door open and step inside. The Oilers score. You hesitate in the doorway. Turn around. Listen to see who it was that scored. The trees in the river valley are a new green. They have been transforming from the gray twigs of winter into this soft, pale nuance. You once knew a woman with eyes this colour. She was a very slender woman. When you lay on top of her, if you weren't careful, you could have cut yourself on her hip bones.

And you remember last spring, when you were in it with Hannah, looking out this window at the trees above the river valley. Black dots scattered like evil Christmas lights in the trees. You got the binoculars and found a murder of crows. A huge murder of crows. A gargantuan murder. Almost a hundred of them in those trees. You stopped counting somewhere near ninety.

The phone is still ringing. You've unplugged and thrown away your answering machine. Ever since your father died you're not interested in what messages people leave. You've saved a message your father left about happiness and a couple of messages from Hannah. Perhaps you've begun to think that nobody really needs answering machines. That they're instruments of the ego. You probably believe that there are very few people so important that they need to be communicated with so desperately. People leaving and picking up messages. People collecting their e-mail. And cell phones? You haven't decided on cell phones. You know many people who are courteous with their phones. And there have been times when you've wished for a cell phone. Once when you met a grizzly on the trail north of Banff you thought it would have been good to have access to emergency services. But the grizzly went his way and you backed down the trail. By making a wide circle around the bear you added three arduous kilometres to your hike. You're not even sure you were close enough to a tower for a cell phone to have worked.

"Hello," you say, finally picking up the receiver.

"You should come."

"When?"

"This weekend."

"It's all right?"

"Yes. I want you to come. Bring your boots. I'm to remind you to bring your boots."

Almost everyone you know talks about how love gets better as it ages. Some people have told you that love doesn't even really get going until you've been married or living with each other for six or seven years. Relationships are like wine, they say. The romantic end falls off and is replaced by something more mature, more even, more exquisite. Really? you say. What could possibly be good about losing romance? You find this trade-off to be an absurd notion.

You've known Sidney for six years. You met at a wedding. It only took a few months for you to become good friends. Then you were at her wedding.

Today, Sidney has straight, black hair and dark-rimmed glasses. Tomorrow, she might show up blond, with green contact-lenses. The next day, she could be a curly red-head in a mini-mini-skirt. The woman was a mood chameleon on steroids. Most people you know will dress according to how they feel that day. For Sidney, that trait was amplified. You really had to focus when you were meeting Sidney. You never knew what she was going to show up as. The thing is, she always pulled it off, made it work. When she dressed up she didn't look dressed up. Come to think of it, you're not sure what Sidney really looks like.

When she walks into the restaurant, a Czech bistro that serves fried breaded cheese, heads turn. She's striking, a tall woman in a pale green pantsuit, and three-inch heels. She orders champagne, insists that you join her.

Sidney is a big advocate of long-term relationships. So are you, within reason. You've just not been lucky yet.

"Let me get this straight," you say. "The trade-off here is mature love for romance? The two don't co-exist?"

"Romance fades," Sidney says. She's been married for four years and she's speaking out of that experience. "Romantic love isn't something we choose. When we're 'in love' we really haven't made any choices. We're just following our crotches, our desires. Our need to mate."

She blushes ever so slightly at her own words.

"Really?" You're astounded by how simple she makes it sound. You hear a small seed of condescension in her tone. Is she lecturing you?

"At some point in your relationship, probably a point you haven't reached yet if you don't know about it, you begin to make the choice to love."

"Really."

"Yes, really. I choose to love Dwayne. I chose to love him."

"And if I was to say, fall in love, would I not also have choices? I either choose to act or I choose not to act."

"Sure, but…"

"…and I'd probably put my morals into action to make those decisions?"

"Well, sure. Look, all I'm saying is that there's a love that has nothing to do with sex, and it's mature and beautiful."

She's placing her experience of love above mine, you think.

"Just as long as you're happy," you say.

"I am. I'm very happy loving Dwayne. I'm very happy in my marriage."

"…even though romance goes right out the window? You're content to live without romance?"

"Yes. Well, no. Not really. It just becomes less important."

"You're a woman for God's sake! Isn't romance everything? Goddamned Cinderella! Snow White! Prince Charming! All those women's magazines! Emotion, emotion, emotion!!!! And never any responsibility for your goddamned emotions! You can't be a real woman." Several people in the restaurant look over at you because you have a big voice, even when it isn't raised.

"Don't be an ass," she whispers. "There's still romance. It's just not everything it was in the beginning."

"So there's still a glimmering of romance in the mix somewhere."

"Well, ya, of course," she says. "You remember it."

"A memory of romance."

"Yes."

"So, mundane drudgery, complacency and a scant memory of romance. And you're happy with that?"

"I'm very happy. Where did you get such a dim view of long-term relationships?"

"My parents, actually. They proved to me that in this day and age it's quite unrealistic to expect people to stay together for life. If we only lived to be thirty or forty years old like a thousand years ago, well, it might be different. But today, marriage is not a realistic arrangement."

"Oh my God, you should stay single."

You smile. "Well, so far so good."

You clink your champagne glasses together. Friendship is a valuable thing. And it becomes more and more valuable as you get older. You remember the old saying that in order to have a friend you must close one eye. And in order to keep a friend, you must close both.

It's a miracle that Sidney doesn't run into more furniture, or walls, or small dogs when she is around you.

"I'm very happy," she said. "I'm *very* happy."

You think perhaps the lady doth protest too much.

Perhaps you were impressed with yourself for being in a tryst with the art critic for your city's biggest daily paper. Could that be it? And what about her art? She'd had shows of her sculptures around the world. Toronto, Montreal, New York, Australia and the list goes on and on. Her art appealed to you. The fact she made art. The fact she was an established artist appealed to you.

When she left, she left a recent work in process. It was a horse, bird, and woman gargoyle. A horrible, frightening thing that was too large to move. She'd muttered something about it being an interesting colour of red, a shade she hadn't expected, thanked you for taking care of it and then she was gone. It was her way to never explain a piece.

And you? You wrote short stories and sent them out. Collected rejection slip after rejection slip from the mailbox. Occasionally, somebody would take one and that would be just enough to drive you to keep going. In the summer, you worked for a landscaping outfit. You built gardens, mostly ugly things. You tried to add a spiritual element to whatever you did but certain garden gnomes and ceramic jockeys often got in your way. Spiritual isn't the right word but it's close. It wasn't exactly spiritual, or feng shui, or mystical, you were after. Rather, it was a kind of unspoken, hazy beauty that perhaps only worked in the rain, or at five a.m., or in the fall for two weeks. There were a couple of gardens every year that thrilled you. A client with vision or a client who awarded freedom of design would come along. With these gardens, you would become obsessed. Problems with space, or light, and finding the exactly right tree or plant would haunt you. Stone placements tormented you. You would spend weeks placing and replacing, placing and adjusting a single rock. Walking around that rock, you would imagine it under three feet of snow, in the fall surrounded by colour, in the summer with new growth, in the rain. And the sun? What does the sun do to the face of the stone in the morning? In the evening? Where do the shadows come? Often, you would finish a job and then come back to the garden three months later with a Bobcat to adjust even a single rock placement.

In the winter, you try to find contract writing work with the government, with the telephone companies and oil companies, with whoever will pay you to write.

In September, you return to the mountains. It could be that you've just come down from a hike up to the Fitzwilliam Basin. Perhaps you're on your way back to the city when you stop in Jasper–seek out Frannie, although you do not yet know her name. The snow is early this year. The ski hills will open in a week. In the meantime, the small town is in the doldrums in between seasons. You stay in the same hotel. Walk slowly through creaky hallways. The pattern in the carpet, a brown and tan and black paisley, is something you do not remember. You wait a long time in the room. You were not so obsessed that you insisted on the same room but this one has almost the same view. Luck put you in this room, not your obsession. You sit on the bed and gaze out the window. Down below are the bear-proof garbage bins in the alleyway and long weaving lines of car tracks in the slushy snow. A whiskey jack alights in a pine tree, someone old walks gingerly with bags of groceries scaled in both hands, a small kid with her coat undone walking home from school.

"There used to be a woman with the dog," you say. You sit at the bar. You try to keep your voice light but not so light that it shows that you're trying to keep it light.

Tammy doesn't really look at you. She half-glances at your face. Is she checking you out to see if you look friendly? To see if you can be trusted with personal information?

"You mean Frannie?"

"She owns a golden retriever."

"Yup, that's Frannie." This woman has a tattoo on her left earlobe. You can't help staring at it. It looks like a small, delicate stained glass window.

"Frannie then. When's her shift?"

"She's gone. What are you drinking?"

You're stunned. Is everything about your time with Hannah to exist only in your own untrustworthy memory?

"Beer."

Tammy looks at you, a sort of side-ways sad look on her face, like she doesn't want to ask you what type of beer; like she does not want to recite the litany of beer brands for you to choose from. She looks at you like you should just know better. A hopeful lifting of her eyebrows.

"Heineken," you say. "Please."

She pulls the fridge open and selects the green bottle, places it on a rubber pad, opens it. She puts the bottle and a frosted glass on the counter in a seemingly reckless way. But you can see that the glass and the bottle are placed perfectly on the counter. There is a sort of pulchritude to the placement. It can't be chance that the label is facing you, that the glass, now sweating, is placed exactly in the center of the coaster. The bottle is slightly back from the glass, creating an angle away from where you sit. A pool of halogen light on the counter gives the placement its finishing touch. You think about Japanese gardens, about stone placements. This woman is a natural. You look down the bar. It feels comfortable, clean. You can imagine this woman's house. A balance of energy and colour. Great light. Light. There's more light in here! This woman has opened up windows, or cleaned them, something. It's very different from when the other woman, Frannie, was here. Of course it's different. Then, you were at the end of something, you were so in love you were pathetic and didn't care. Now, you're drifting, trying not to recapture, beginning to almost unravel the mystery. You want to understand how something like this could have happened. You're looking at your bruises and wondering if there's internal bleeding. You don't normally drink beer from a glass but Tammy, because of her careful placement, has coerced you into considering it.

"She quit," Tammy says. "Two weeks ago. She left town."

You have no idea what you would have said to this Frannie woman anyway. Something in you remembers an odd connection. An uncomfortable feeling between the two of you. Perhaps, you think, if you can see Frannie, Hannah will magically appear upstairs. She'll be lying on the bed, naked, reading a newspaper when you go up. You'll crawl into bed with her. Lean against the wall with her head in your lap. And you'll read the newspaper together. Or she'll continue to read the newspaper and you'll find something interesting in the book bag. And at some point, Hannah will roll over and gently take you in her mouth. She'll make it seem normal. Like it's nothing. And you'll keep reading. You won't stop reading. You might read the same line over and over but you won't stop reading. There'll be a slow-moving innocence that drifts timeless. A loveliness inside this willingness to please.

"She didn't leave a forwarding address. But I heard …" She pauses. Looks at you fully. "…why did you want to find her?"

"I didn't say I wanted to find her. I was just wondering where she was."

"Oh, ya. Well, she's working up at the Elk Pasture now, at the Hot Springs. That's what I heard." Tammy places another perfect bottle of beer on the counter in front of you. She twists it slightly, pulls a new glass from the freezer, places it beside the bottle.

pulchri|tude (-kr-) n. (literary). beauty: hence ~tud inous

pukka, -ah a. (Anglo-Ind.) of full weight: genuine; permanent, solidly built

So you would actually consider going after Hannah and embracing the mundane? What the hell are you thinking? Are you mad? Get on with your life for Christ's sake. Find someone to love who's available. Find someone who can love you without guilt. The whole thing was idiotic. There, you see? It "was" idiotic. Put it in the past and you'll be fine. Do you think you actually knew Hannah? Do you know what it's like to wake up with her day after day after day, for years at a time? Does she have morning breath? What does she look like when she's peeing? How does she brush her teeth? Do her feet smell when she wears cheap shoes? You don't know anything about the mundane Hannah. All your experiences with her have been extraordinary. Think about that before you even consider trundling off to the east coast to be with her.

But it's my heart, you say to yourself. There's a problem with my heart.

You're nervous when you go to mail the first poem. All your insecurities rise up and make themselves weighty. There is a possibility that these poems could come back unopened. Like e-mails sometimes bounce back at you when the address isn't exactly right. You're not using e-mail with Hannah. E-mail is too instant. You're not even sure she has e-mail. You want the wait. You want the scratching of the pen on paper. You want all the tactile pleasures of writing a letter. There is something frivolous about e-mail. Letters written on paper, even if the envelopes contain only crappy little heart-written poems, have a gravity to them.

So you seal up your first poem, lick the stamp and walk out of your office, down on to the street to find a mailbox.

Perhaps you walk around downtown looking for the right mailbox. It has to feel right. You're not sure what that mailbox is going to have that all the others are missing but you trust yourself to know it when you see it.

Under a spreading elm, beside a red-brick apartment block is the mail box you decide on. A massive sense of relief that floods over you when you drop that first envelope.

Seconds after your relief, you know you do not ever want to finish this campaign. It is too cathartic to stop.

(1)
Tree

I would rather have you here and now
with sorrow held true and dark

I would love you
with all I understand of being
with every nuance of the poetry in between

I would love you with all of floundering desire
with no thing bridled

I would surrender all protection,
abandon armor, open myself

I would open as this tree opens
on this dismal spring day
with innocence and trust and faith

I would greet each new day as this tree does—
surprised at its own green
touched by the slow warmth
happy for the dwindling blackness
and delighted by uncertain, chaotic bird song

If you were here
I would open my leaves and live

Are you a romantic? Well, look at the facts. You had an affair with a woman who has kids. This is a woman who had just left her husband. Something in you decided to forget the husband. Forget the kids. Forget that she planned to go to the east coast and reconnect with her husband, live as a family. Forget that it was over before it started. It was ending as it was beginning. The end was folded over the beginning. Most sane people would have turned away. Said to themselves: There's nothing here for me but grief. But not you. You decide to take that journey right to the end. Because you never know. Life is crazy. It's supposed to be crazy. So you have hope. Even though Hannah and you have talked honestly about what she is going to do, you have hope.

The dictionary should read: *romantic: 1) person with a stupid heart 2) you.*

You never meet Michelle but after the dam bursts and Frannie talks about what happened on the mountain, you learn quite a bit about her. They hung out at the Bistro together, Frannie says. It's not hard for you to imagine them there. You're surprised you don't remember seeing them.

It's not hard for you to see them sitting there, perhaps in the corner. Just a few scattered customers. There's a man in the corner who keeps clearing his throat. A grating sound. Perhaps he doesn't notice he's doing it. Another man at the front of the Bistro, out of sight around the corner, is talking very loudly on a cell phone about some stocks he wants to buy but he wants to keep quiet about. There is always classical music playing. Tonight it is snowing heavily, drifting past the front window. The snow mixes with bundled people, slow cars, and darkness. It spares no one. Falls with a keen white democracy. The ancient cranky heaters at the front push warmth throughout the room but complain noisily with occasional loud bouts of thumping. People coming in, stomp their shoes at the front entrance, shake their coats. The service is perfectly European. Waiters and waitresses who learn their customers, who watch carefully and have an eye for the smallest details. Dark, wooden tables and chairs, lamps with elegant, ivory-coloured shades. It is always romantic to be in the Bistro while it's snowing. The light across the street becomes a translucent mystery. And the snow sifting past the front window is a frail pleasure.

Frannie has come into the city to shop. It pains her a bit to see Michelle but they have common memories. They have a bond that few people on the planet have. Frannie is keenly aware that Michelle has secrets. There are hidden alcoves in Michelle. But the bond between them jumps any gap with ease.

When Franto comes in, he sees them and smiles. Two beautiful women in the back corner of his bistro. Why wouldn't he smile? He removes his coat, a light-coloured fur of some sort, wolf perhaps, and hat, a fox with tail still attached, and shakes the snow from them. He's a big man, tall, with a wide girth. Apart from his belly and dramatic goatee, his enormous appetite for champagne is his most distinguishable outward trait. The volume of champagne he consumes is quite astounding. And there are exquisitely simple methods for drinking champagne, which Franto adheres to without faltering.

Michelle pushes a handful of blond hair behind her right ear. She looks across the room. Watches in small awe as Franto moves smoothly behind the bar and picks a bottle of champagne out of the fridge. He arrives at their table with the bottle and three flutes.

"May I join you, ladies?" he asks.

"We'd be honoured," Frannie says.

"On the contrary, I am the one who is…" A rumbling sound comes from deep within his stomach cavity. "…well, ummmm…honoured." He pushes his hand towards Frannie. She places her hand in his and Franto kisses it with an unexpected gentleness. He repeats this gesture with Michelle and then without fuss, pops the cork and sits down.

"How are you, Franto?" Michelle says.

"I am…you know…ummmm, well, you know, quite pissed,"

he says as he pours. "But happy. Happy to be alive, and in the company, of such beautiful women." Well-used, tired lines but Franto's charm shines through. He could recite the phonebook, if he could read it, and still be certifiably charming. He sells these lines like a Shakespearean actor delivering one of the great soliloquies. Then he unfurls a smile that is both charming and wicked.

A week later, around midnight, you go to the Bistro for a cognac. But Franto sits at your table with a bottle of champagne and two glasses and begins to talk about life, about art, about love, about opera, about women. You practice the *Czech Standing Column of Pleasure*, a secret method of drinking champagne that you have to this day not come close to mastering. The champagne keeps magically appearing, and around 4:30 a.m., long after all other customers have gone home and the waitresses have cashed out, Franto turns to you and delivers a beautiful epigram of his life. He does not deliver this line with his usual bravado. It is just sad and flat and true. "People," he says, "People are always telling me they are worried about my drinking…that I drink too much. But no one ever asks me how thirsty I am."

You were never there with Hannah. Even though you sometimes feel that you almost live at the Bistro, you never met Hannah there. You have no memories of Hannah sitting at the table in the corner, or behind the liquor credenza.

You know Franto very well. You've spent a great deal of time listening to him. And over the years you've grown to love his Zorba soul. You are not one of the people who are worried about Franto's drinking. You like it that he is a bon vivant, a dreamer, an artist and a flirt. But there has never been any doubt in your mind that he drinks too much.

Each poem you send is a cruelty, a small barb, and a torment. But you do not think about that. You just have to send them. You have to deliver the message of your heart to Hannah and you do not think about the consequences of that message.

The mountains have to work very hard in order to be seen and heard over your gloominess. The larches are golden lemon pockets amidst the vastness of pine. The grasses in the valleys are hunched and brown. The elk are in rut. You hear them at night with their high-pitched, longing sirens of need. Fall is your favorite season in the mountains but its beauty barely registers.

So you know where this Frannie woman is. You had no clue as to why you wanted to find her in the first place. Perhaps it was as simple as creating a physical link to some part of Hannah. Hannah barely saw Frannie when you were here. It was you who made the connection. You were alone when you made the connection yet Frannie remains a memory touchstone to Hannah.

You tuck away Frannie's location and try to get on with your life. You do not intend to follow her. Tammy said her name. That's enough for now. If Frannie exists, then so does Hannah. You have your proof. Frannie is at the Elk Pasture, at the hot springs. You do not intend to go there. But you do not have a good record of adhering to your intentions.

Extrapolate. What if in a year you still don't know. It's mid-summer and you still don't know. The pangs of desire for Hannah will have receded slightly. Sure, that's normal. But your stomach still churns when you think of her. You've sent her the fifty-two poems and she has written you a few sweet yet convoluted letters back. Now what?

You find yourself attracted to women who are single and have kids. Some part of you that you don't understand is drawn to these women. Perhaps you want to see what could have been. Perhaps you feel guilt about Hannah's husband. What the hell is his name? Why can't you remember his name? It isn't Norm. But for some reason you want to call him that. Norm will have to do.

But you have always been attracted to women who have had children. Is there something finished about them? Not every woman who has had children is appealing to you. It's the women who manage to maintain their identity as human beings while, at the same time, being mothers. Some of these women are attracted to you too. There must be a kind of tragedy in your eyes, a sadness on the surface of your skin. Some women are attracted to men who seem to need mothering. Some are attracted, you've noticed, to men who seem to need nothing. And some women are very attracted to anything damaged. You were not aware of the damage in you. Not yet.

Do you want to know what that damage is? Here's a hint. The four months you were with Hannah were the most thrilling, titillating four months of your life. You were almost constantly in a panting state of desire, suspended above the ground by sexual adrenaline, dizzy and unstrung.

Here's another hint. You miss that intensity. It's as if there is a hole in you that cannot be mended.

But is that all? Is that everything? Desire, passion, sex. What about the meeting of the parts of the soul that makes an artist an artist? The artist in you met a partner. And at the end of the four months? Was there something else? See? Even sitting in your Bistro, drinking your third cup of coffee, you look away from the end. You look away from your own history. You deny your own story.

desire[1] (-z-) n. unsatisfied longing, feeling that one would derive pleasure or satisfaction from attaining or possessing something; expression of this, request: thing desired; lust or craving b. an expression of this; a request 2. sexual appetite, lust 3. something desired

What is she thinking about as she drives across this country? You can only guess. Perhaps she feels a slow release of the burden of this intensity. A relief which moves like the colour of the sky in the morning as she drives towards the sunrise. Deep indigo moves to navy blue. Navy blue moves to periwinkle. Periwinkle moves to pale blue. Pale blue moves to cool orange moves to butter yellow, moves to sunlight in her eyes and looking away.

Does her life become more simple? Less messy? Is there peace at the end of this road? Or is there just more chaos?

She still has her inner mania. The thing that fuels her art. Calm on the outside but manic inside. Now, her mania is focused not on you, but instead, on the road. She has a lot of driving to do before she can rest.

Perhaps she is asking herself questions. What have I been doing? What am I doing? Are her daughters with her? Do they demand her attention and time?

Or perhaps she is thinking about the size of this country. Driving across a country produces a connected understanding of its immensity. Across this country, there is such vast space. In between pockets of clustered humans there is sufficient time and space to feel horribly alone.

You don't care what Hannah's thinking as she drives. You wish safety for her. And you wish her happiness. You've just moved into a new flat that is comprised of the main floor of an old house. There are boxes everywhere. You don't have the will to unpack. Not right now. You unpack two boxes. Pour yourself a drink of whiskey. The phone is not hooked up yet but you unplug it anyway. You light candles. Turn off the lights. You walk around your flat with a roll of black electrical tape. You tape all the light switches down. Decide to live with candles for a while.

Oh, of course you care what's she's thinking. You hope she's thinking about you. Why do you lie to yourself like that? You want Hannah to dwell on you at times when she should be focused elsewhere. You'd like it if she was fucked up about leaving. You'd like it if she missed that exit in Saskatoon. Or if she got on the wrong highway in Winnipeg. Or if she just ran out of gas in rural Ontario somewhere. You want her to feel the way you do.

(3)
Highway

I am thinking about you   WHILE I'm,
in this old house   AND there is,
                    con   f
usion
                                        around me, (boxes, pil
                    ed on
  to   p of box
 es pile   d o   n top   of
                         box   e   s
goddamned boxes filled up with my life(?)   AND YOU,
are on a highway somewhere on the prairies in the middle of
S   a   s   k   a   t   c   h   e   w   a   n
flat, dry, and brown from three weeks of heat and no rain   YOU,
are lugging a big trailer to The East   YOU,
are pulling your life away from me   AND I,
in this   (m)@#%^&*()(((+
* $ (e) %   ***** &&
&*^$#   %%%%%   (((s)
                         ))^^^+@@@@$!!!!!!   (s),
not wanting to look,
inside any of these often-moved boxes   INSTEAD I,
will make a quiet place of peace, a small sanctuary somewhere,
and think about you on the prairie, Styrofoam coffee in hand,
squinting into the   flat   dark   night
AND I will,
very miss you

four

"I yearn for the aspects of you"

Noreen is not Hannah. What did you expect? Surely you didn't expect her to be anything like Hannah. Although she has recently left her husband, and has two children, she is not Hannah. Noreen's husband's name is George. You know this because she talks about George a great deal. George was not interested in getting Noreen back into his life. He was finished with her except for the kids.

"My ex, George, was an avid golfer. He loved to golf. He loved to watch golf. I can't imagine anything more boring that watching golf on television! You don't golf do you?"

"No, I don't golf. I've tried it a few times but I just didn't like it." The lies we'll tell to get someone into the sack! Men are despicable, you think. You love golf. You love being out in the open air early in the morning. You love the creaking velocity of the game. You love the fact that it's the only time you actually feel like drinking beer that early in the morning, and when you do have a beer you feel no guilt about it.

"And last Christmas, he neglected to pick the kids up for Christmas. They sat around all day waiting for him. He just didn't come!"

"Jesus, you can't do that to kids." You find out later that he'd been stuck in central British Columbia because of avalanches on the Trans-Canada. He'd phoned several times to explain.

You systematically try to accentuate the differences between you and Noreen's ex. It's the mating dance. You show your good side, she shows hers. When it comes right down to it, you weren't that much different from George. You love sitting down in front of the television with a beer and watching a hockey game. Not every single hockey game on television but perhaps as many as three or four a month.

You meet Noreen in the fall at an office party you'd have rather skipped. You're in a small ballroom. They called it the *small ballroom* in the invitation. A small ballroom! You looked at those words a couple of times. A beautiful contradiction, you think. The hotel is elegant. It sits on edge of the river valley and has been there in one form or another as long as the city. She comes after you with a bottle of pretty good red wine, wanting to talk. She appears to know a lot about wine. Asks questions to which you supply half-hearted, aloof answers. Noreen is not dismayed.

"I'm not usually so forward but you look a little sad and so I thought I'd come over and share this wine with you. You're not sad are you? Do you want to be alone because..."

"...You're attracted to sad-looking people are you?"

"Oh I didn't say I was attracted to you. I'm just trying to be friendly. People say I'm quite friendly. Some even say I'm really quite nice. Did Frank say you were a writer and a gardener? Well, this wine is particularly good and I'd like to share it with a writer-gardener. It's Australian. I'm a bit of a wine snob. I've been known to say that wine only comes from one country." She laughs, a quick, warm giggle-laugh. "N'est pas?"

"Germany?" you say, which makes her giggle even more. You happen to agree with her. To hear this verbose woman speak your own thoughts makes you smile. In your mind, France is the only country for wine.

She pours you a glass. Is she looking for a wedding ring or is she admiring the colour of the wine? Perhaps both, you decide.

Regardless, she is not looking you in the eye. The wine is not subtle. But the temperature is right.

"My name is…"

"…I know who you are," she says. "I mean, I know your name. I was paying attention earlier. I'm Noreen. Pleased to meet you."

You're not one of those people who judge other people by the way they shake hands. But if you were, Noreen would rate highly for firmness. Her hand is narrow and dry and strong. She holds your hand for just the right amount of time. Looks you in the eye when she does it. She has blue eyes. A strange navy blue. Something else in there too. Hazel?

At this point, you don't know she's getting divorced and has two kids. You're unaware of the pattern you're flying. But you are attracted to her. You want to get to know her. What makes her tick? What are her stories? That's all. You want to learn her. Eventually, you find out about her. But you also find out about George. You hear about all of George's failings. Do women talk about their ex-lovers' failings in bed? You'd like to think not. But they do sometimes. And sometimes you don't want to hear. Sidney used to talk about how big her boyfriend's penis was. He was an ex-CFL football player who'd spent time in jail for trafficking. It was around the time when you two flirted with the idea of going out. "It was huge," she'd say. "It was so big that it was almost unmanageable. My God! I've never felt anything like that when he was inside me." You find talk like this disconcerting. Perhaps she did it on purpose, to sabotage any chance of getting together with you.

Hannah never talked about…What the hell is his name? She never talked about their sex together. There was something wrong hidden back there, something in her sexual make-up, beyond any experience with her husband.

Noreen talks a great deal about how awful sex was with George. You're pretty sure she doesn't mean "filled with awe!"

"He got me to wear masks when we made love. You know, like Halloween. Marilyn Monroe, Richard Nixon, or Casper the Friendly Ghost, it didn't matter. And he liked it when I wasn't so clean. He was a smell freak. He was always sniffing my armpits. I mean, God! The smell of my armpits turned him on! And my shoes. He liked it when my feet were smelly. He was so weird."

And you listen and shake your head and think, well, the smell of a woman's armpits, it sort of turns me on too. You read an article that said there were pheromones in that smell. Nothing she tells you about George's sexual leanings shocks you or disturbs you. You just really do not want to know.

Did you consider making love with Noreen? Yes, of course, you were headed down that path. She was a big-boned woman. You couldn't say she was fat. Her body was voluptuous and sexy. There was a fluidity to it. Noreen was also a lingerie addict. She had lingerie in every colour and every imaginable variation. She never went out in a dress without nylons and a garter belt. And she loved to kiss. She kissed recklessly and hard. Yes, you were slowly moving towards making love with her.

You noticed her garter belt, and nylons that first night. Nylons with a strange pattern on them. White, everything was white. You were meant to notice. The glimpse of Noreen's lingerie as her dress was hiked up in an awkward gesture of sitting down was planned and well executed. But with that small peek, you hadn't even begun to understand the extent of the exotic adventure into which you were being drawn.

(15)
I yearn for the aspects of you

I do not remember specifically
only vaguely do I recall
sutras of conversation
reckless pleasure with room service
potent clusters of loving
the comfort of a deep valley
becoming lost,
in a room at the top of the stairs, with you
Miles Davis, trees, benches,
simply walking

whiskey and spring water after loving
your certain touch
your intense gait through forests
Finding you held just above the floor—
suspended by Bach's double violin concerto in D minor
The gravity of you pulling—
pulling me perfectly off course
Absolute lust-love
because each minute is a beginning
because each minute is the end

All this is alive because
I squint my eyes
let the pictures become fuzzy
blur with purpose
I do not go to the past
but instead, wait for past to visit
I cultivate a jazz memory
begin with a theme
digress, fold, twirl it tango orange
and taciturn blue and under-robin red

there is always one thing more
to remember
and at the heart

there are the aspects
of you.

Can human beings love more than one person at a time?

How could you possibly consider making love to another woman only four months after Hannah? Four months. Roughly sixteen poems. Four months of her being away. Four months of very little contact. It wasn't so hard to imagine sleeping with a new woman. There was something steady between you and Hannah. You imagined it would always be there, regardless of who you slept with, who you loved, or who you lived with. Like the two of you had lived through some disaster and now there was an unshakable bond. You feel a little invincible. As if you could walk through the valley of love and lust with impunity. You will always have Hannah.

So you've become a bit of an oxymoron. With one hand you pen these love poems to Hannah, and then you place your other hand on your chin and consider sleeping with Noreen. It raises a lot of questions.

Most people you know would have taken some time off. Perhaps, you should have immersed yourself in your work. It would have been smarter if you had just ignored all women for a good long time. But you needed to figure it out. At least that's what you thought you needed. So you kept yourself open to new connections. You didn't actively search but you kept the door open. And things happened. You got to tell your story to different people. And for the most part you were not alone.

In reality, you were frantic to make a connection at the Hannah level again. And you were lonely.

Do you know anybody in your life who's steady and faithful and happy in a relationship?

You meet Sidney at the Bistro. You're late. And she does not look happy.

"I'm sorry," you say. "Got held up in a meeting."

"It's fine." She gulps down the entire glass of the cheap-ass champagne you usually drink and then waits for a small burp before refilling her glass. This champagne-method wine was cheaper than beer.

"What's up?"

"I don't want to talk about it…"

"…which is the reason you called me, the reason you wanted to meet?"

"I really don't want to talk about it. Just thought I'd have a couple drinks with you."

"Jesus, you're acting like, well, you're acting like me. It's usually me who won't talk about what's bugging me, not you. Now, what's going on? What causes you to drink like a fish in the middle of a Tuesday afternoon?

"Nothing."

"Are you angry at me about something?"

"No."

"Is it something with you and Dwayne?"

She gulps another full glass and doesn't wait for the burp before filling her glass. "I think he's having an affair." Then the burp comes, loud and bold. "S'cuse me," she adds.

"You're sure?"

"No, I'm not sure. That's why I said *'I think'*. I just can't believe this could happen to me."

"So, what are the signs? What makes you 'think' he's fooling around on you? Really, I don't think Dwayne would…"

"…oh cut the crap. You men always stick together don't you."

"Well, what are the signs?"

"Oh, I know," she says.

"What do you mean you know?"

"I know the signs."

"How do you know?"

"I know the goddamned signs because I've been screwing around on him for two years."

What if Hannah's not keeping track? What if she has no idea that you're sending her a poem every week for a year? Well, really, how could she know the time frame? Poems start arriving. You send them to her work address. Sometimes you courier them. Most times you send them regular mail.

You can imagine her picking up the envelopes and putting them in a pocket. A recognition of the writing on the envelope—the beginning movements of a symphony of anticipation. Perhaps she would carry them for weeks until the light was right, or the clouds were a certain pallid density. Or until she'd had enough scotch to dull the initial prick of opening the envelopes. Perhaps she always waited until it rained.

She would only notice that the poems stopped. Perhaps she would be having a bath late at night, after the kids were settled in bed, and something would dawn on her. Candles beside the tub making the water reflection dance on the wall. A hollow echo swishing sound. She's reading the last poem she received. Looking for a clue as to why there have been no more. She reads it over and over. There are no clues. A poem about glaciers and how they move. But we are not moving, she'll think. Or, we are moving only it's too slow to see. No, don't think that this poem is about you. That is too much ego. Just look at the poem as a poem. Nothing more, nothing less.

She gulps red wine from a coffee mug. Thinks about when they began. A year, she thinks. He gave me a year of his life beyond where I expected to have him. I've been hiking with him. We've been on the sides of mountains. I've been grieving with him. I've yearned along with him. Now what? Do I encourage this connection? Do I still have him? I wonder, does he still have me?

(19)
The Moon and you

I cannot look at the moon
without thinking of you far away
under the same pale globe

last night as the Earth eclipsed the moon
it was a shadow across your face
and precisely something in me reached out to you

perhaps you were watching the same lunar covering
and uncovering, this slow shadow journey
easy to imagine you crouched
on the front lawn with awakened kids
insisting they should see this because it's
rare and wondrous, and magic
oh ya, you tell them there's magic, mystery
you tell them about the astronomy
and you invoke wonder

it is perhaps a sad thing to write letters to the moon
because she is ruled by an unrepentant gravity
lives in a vacuum of heavenly objects

the moon habitually does not write back
only appears reflected in the quiet pools, slowly in windows
and barely through the branches of certain trees

and the only way I can hold you
is to kneel in the darkness beside a mountain stream
cup cold water in my hands
and lift it up to the night

Noreen gets stranger every time you go out. You are both doing the dance. Peeling back the layers. You're both directing light on to your good parts. But Noreen seems to be incapable of lying. She's blunt and forthright with her feelings and thoughts. You're getting information you wouldn't expect to get so early.

"I'm in debt," she says. "But not too much. I used a line of credit to pay off my student loan and so, the line of credit is maxed out. I can't seem to get far enough ahead to make a dent in it."

"You have to go and get tested. I won't make love with you unless you get tested for HIV. Okay, honey? And then you and I can play." She looks at you and bites her top lip. "And then we can really play."

"I'd like it if you got a tattoo. Nothing too big but something that reminds you of me. Like maybe: 'Property of Noreen Tannas' across your butt at about 72 point." This gets her giggling.

"I have fetishes. Lots and lots of fetishes. I don't know a fetish I haven't, umm, well, tried."

"Sometimes I hate my kids. Sometimes I really wonder what drives the human race to procreate." She looks right through you, then focuses and perhaps notices you're not really looking at her but rather watching two young girls wearing hundred dollar blue jeans begging for money outside a liquor store across the street.

"I'd like it if you stuck a finger up my cunt right now. I want your hand between my legs right now. In my cunt."

Only later do you guess that there were stories you should have uncovered. Once, she started to tell you about being raped when she was very young. Perhaps you were too close to see how damaged she was. Perhaps it was a story she should have told to somebody loving and compassionate.

Sometimes, Noreen was a woman who explained too much, who talked too much. But you're a particularly curious human being. And life, well, life is supposed to be a chaotic mess. Neat and tidy compartments are for accountants and MBAs. Life can go ahead and be all neat and tidy when you're dead. For now, it's all dress rehearsal. Maybe we never get to the goddamned play.

Perhaps there are only special times when Hannah will allow herself to think of you. That's how she does it. She is not like you, with your backwards, jumbled memory. Hannah remembers systematically. As if she is writing a story for the newspaper, she remembers one thing and then asks what is the next logical memory. What do I want to remember next? Perhaps these special times are when she is away from her family. Perhaps they come when she is particularly dislocated by a piece of theatre, or a sunset, or something one of her children says, or does. But she must be moving away from her life when she thinks of you.

Or maybe she only brings out your poems and reads them on the ferry, when the slender line between the breathing ocean and pressing sky is easy to approach. Can you see her sitting there in a window seat, the rain drops scattered on the window pane? A woman with a down-turned face, leaning against the window, one foot up on the edge of her seat. She's tired. Why is she on a ferry? You don't know. Perhaps she's never been on a ferry in her life. Hazard a guess. An assignment perhaps, in Newfoundland? What is there for her in Newfoundland? Maybe she has a friend there. Maybe she has a fondness for moose.

Close your eyes. Can you feel the movement of the ferry? The steady droning hum of the engines far below? Perhaps that's her over there leaning on the railing. See the woman in the yellow slicker? She's looking out to sea. There! See? She dropped a sheet of paper into the water and the ocean swallows it quickly and without notice.

Hazard: n., & v.t. **1.** n. dice game with complicated chances; chance (source of) danger; at ~ (arch.) at random……**3.** expose to hazard; run the risk of; venture on (action, statement, guess).

It was about this time that your father died. You knew about the cancer, of course, and the treatments. You met him each day for a week while he was having chemotherapy treatments and sat with him. You thought of this as just hanging out with your father.

Things seemed to be going all right and then, and then something went terribly wrong and he died.

We all grieve in different ways. That's what the Reverend said to you. Reverend Shaw was his name. A clumsy, gentle, soft-spoken man.

Your way, you begin to discover, would be a slow, meticulous and constant thing. Not ice hockey but baseball. Did your life change? Hmmm. It was as if an angel wearing thick black eyeglasses came down to Earth, took you by the hand and said: "You have to come and stand over here now." And so you follow that angel. This is not some sweet angel from a curio shop filled with kitsch. Imagine a not-so-pleasant angel with gun strapped to its hip. This angel is huge and with all those wings and white lights and heavenly choruses singing, it's difficult *not* to be impressed. It's hard to say no to an angel. Especially this one. You go and stand where the gun-toting angel wants you to stand and you don't really notice a difference. Perhaps it's darker in your new spot. The stars shine brighter. A peculiar intensity. Then the angel says: "There'll be no going back." and then: "I have to go now." And it shakes your hand. You don't know if it's a man angel or a woman angel. It shakes your hand almost exactly like Noreen does. You feel a great deal of wind on your face and the angel is gone. You feel slightly more alone. Certain things that are very important to you come sharply into focus. Stuff. Your processions, your *things* become nearly meaningless. *Things* like television and movies, making a lot of money and certain people, all become floating snippets of dandelion fluff. People around you begin to think you've lost your mind but you feel as sane as you ever have in your whole life.

You wished for Hannah to be there with you. To hold her hand and walk under the dismal emaciated fingers of trees. Walk along streets stranded beneath snow skies. Or to walk on a country road with snow all packed down. Listen to the squeaking, crunching sound your boots make. You don't even know if Hannah would have been capable of giving you the comfort you needed. You only hoped she was.

Right after the funeral, voices in your heart start to demand to know what you're doing with your life. They want to know who you love. They want to know who you care about. They're asking about your bliss.

You just want to get laid, or drunk, or both. You always want something that makes you feel alive after a funeral. This day, you do not have the opportunity to make love. And there is no one with whom you'd like to drink. So you re-visit a garden you'd worked on the previous summer. You want to see how it looks with two feet of snow.

You do not go into the stale basement of the church for insipid coffee served from tall silver silos. You do not go down there to accommodate people's awkwardness. As you are leaving the church two children run up the stairs screaming with glee, chasing each other, laughing. An older woman with dyed black hair turns and yells after them to shush. "Be quiet," she shouts, "No running. Be quiet."

You only meet Noreen's kids once. Rebecca and Marnie. Six and seven. Or was it seven and eight? She was the good protective mother. You were introduced as a friend from work.

You never met Hannah's kids. You imagine Hannah treats them with respect and tolerance. She would probably go out of her way to make their eyes open in wonder as often as possible. Can you see her with the girls in their pajamas, standing in the front yard, the grass all dewy and cool? She's explaining what a lunar eclipse is. She's telling them the story of what they're about the witness. She'll fill them with a mythology of her own devising, and with science. And they'll remember this night. They'll remember the arching shadow moving across the moon. This night will sit there like a dream just under the surface of their skin for the rest of their lives. They will not be shallow, narrow-focused children. They'll know about the world, and the heavens, about art and love.

You would never imagine in a thousand thousand years that Frannie and Nick would wind up working together. How could you know Nick owned the Elk Pasture Resort, along with his brother Costas? Frannie met Nick at the Chickadee. After too much red wine one night, she told him she was looking for a new place to work. She needed a change. She needed to not work so damned hard. She needed a place to heal. Nick, of course, knew all about the accident. He followed what went on in the park regarding climbs very closely. He knew most of the details of that tragedy. He still had a rabid enthusiasm for the peaks. Now, at sixty-three, major climbs were only daydreams. Although with the right team, he could still hold his own. Nick hiked and scrambled as much as he could. The Elk Pasture was nestled at the edge of the park with nearly unlimited climbing opportunities. It also happened to be a two-minute walk from the Hot Springs. Nick offered Frannie a position in the dining room and lodging for the season. The dog was no problem.

"Can you make a Greek coffee?" he'd asked.

"Set you on your ass," Frannie said.

"Good." He smiles and nods his head. "Good."

It can't be her but you squint your eyes and try to determine if it is. Why would she be here, in this Safeway, now? It makes no sense. Your heart is beating triple. She would have called or written, or something. Hannah's in Montreal right now. Her last letter said she was in Montreal, working on a play about Miles Davis. You know that. You think you know that. And then something irrational in you decides it doesn't matter if this is Hannah or not. You have to talk to this woman. You have to hear her voice. Perhaps you can get close enough to smell her.

She went up there, towards the bakery. All right, move along the back of the store towards where she was headed. Check up aisles as you go. Is that…no that's not her. My god, it looked just like Hannah.

When you arrive in the bread section, she's gone. You practically run through this end of the store, walk the front of the store looking at line-ups, and up and down aisles. The impostor is nowhere to be seen. You've lost her twice, you think. And then: Jesus, that's idiotic. It wasn't her. What the hell is wrong with you?! You turn around and stumble over your own feet, fall into a Wagon Wheel pyramid. You wind up on the floor, on your back, with small boxes avalanched around you. Someone's offering a hand. Her! She's offering her hand. She's asking you something.

"Are you okay?"

Take her hand you idiot! Take it!

So you take her hand and she helps you up. Her voice is different, deeper, smoother. Her eyes are hazel and slightly further apart.

"I'm sorry," you say.

"Why?" She smiles. A big, gummy smile. "It happens."

"I wasn't paying attention. I, I was looking for someone, I was looking for you."

"Me?"

"Yes, you remind me of someone I know. Ummm, I knew."

"Oh?"

What's she thinking? Is she thinking this is a lame, lame attempt at picking somebody up? Does she think you're a sleaze?

"In fact, at first, I really thought you were her," you say.

"She must have been something. I think I might like it that someone was moved enough to destroy a Wagon Wheel display over me." She smiles again and then she adds that she has to be going. She wishes you luck with finding whoever it is you're really looking for and also with your walking. You stay briefly to apologize for knocking over the display and then you skulk out of the store.

Are you the same unnerving distraction for Hannah that she is for you?

You do not imagine Hannah waking up in the morning to make breakfast, to get the kids off to school. You do not have a domestic image of her. As much as you'd like to go there, you can't get past the memory of her mouth, the curve of her hip, her scent. An ongoing dialogue like bullets wedged somewhere in the sinews of a metaphor. Inoperable and lovely. Domestic life is not intrinsically romantic. You cannot picture a domestic Hannah but she must be. In one of her realities she must be.

Hannah almost sees you at a small jazz festival in St. John's, Newfoundland. She loses her breath, sits down and watches your almost-doppelganger until she is certain it is not you. Would he do this? she asks herself. Yes. It's like him to come without saying. Perhaps her husband is there beside her. Asks her what's wrong. "The heat," she says. "I feel a little lightheaded."

Or maybe she looks at that person who resembles you and decidedly looks away. Her heart beats faster not steeped in excitement but rather, terror. Just behind this terror is the fear that she will hurt her husband, again. That this is not good timing. That she's just gotten settled. That she does not have the strength to go through this again. Not right now.

Even hummingbirds land, stop for a while. They require safe places to land—high up in the shadows of pine trees, far back in the forest.

(23)
you

I am lost in a wave of only you
tonight I would place aside the flesh
stop hormone and ego and tactile pleasure
peel away the pink molecules one by one

dis-remember touch, disallow sweetness recalled
deconstruct this haphazardly built castle
rediscover new ways of life
create the words for this grieving,aching,joy
make new languages composed of the silences

all this I would do gladly
for a glimpse of your face,
the leaning timbre of your voice,
the flip of your hair in the check-out line
at Safeway on Tuesday night,
a walk amongst the fall pines in the mountains
on a cloud-hidden day,
a lone word
with you

five

Smyth is still holding out for more money

We all grieve in different ways. You think yours might be aloneness. You should probably be attending the after-funeral gathering at your mother's house. But the gathering will still be there when you've finished your inspection of this garden. Amazing, though, how your mother rallied behind this man, her ex-husband. A phenomenal level of compassion in that woman.

At the garden you can see where you'll have work in the spring. Two Siberian willows need to be moved. They've grown too tall. Two of the stones are wrong. That arrangement of rocks in the corner beside the apple tree is not quite as peaceful as it could be. There are many things that ring true and beautiful. The apple boughs feather out in slender waves. And just now, because there has been no wind today, a small line of snow crests along the tops of branches.

You think about your father. And then Hannah. They never met. You've got your flask. You take a couple of swigs of the scotch and then screw the top on tight. You're feeling a little abandoned. You know that's silly but you're willing to humour anything irrational or illogical right now. What do you have to do in order to keep someone you love in your life? Oh, sure they're still embedded in memory, caught in your heart. You can feel them. But that sort of wispy connection is a far cry from a touch, a hand, a voice. You suddenly feel very lonely.

You've read about Buddhist monks who study for years only to go back into society and become normal. Inside normal is something extraordinary. Inside of them is a profound enlightenment and they look like normal folks. They're out there in the rice fields, or sweeping a street, or taking money from parkers in a parking lot, and inside is an incredible balance, an astounding peace.

The Buddhist monk Thich Nhat Hanh, in his book *Zen Keys*, says, "there is no enlightenment outside daily life." Hannah gave you one of his books called *The Miracle of Mindfulness*. They were good books to take to the mountains. Was she trying to tell you something?

At some point in this story you will hold a woman in your arms who is crying, sobbing about the death of someone. There's been a horrible accident. Someone she loved. And now she loves you. Or is time confused? Is it you who has died? Did you dream this? No, you could not have dreamed your own death. We always wake up just before we die in our dreams. That's how hard we humans cling to this life. Imagine your subconscious becoming conscious, developing a will, thinking or saying: Ah what the hell, let her die tonight. Or: Ahhh, he's depressed anyway, let him die. And in your dream, you die. Do you wake up out of that dream? Is that how people die peacefully in their sleep?

Were you climbing? Did something go wrong? Or will you climb that mountain in the future? There! There it is! You don't recognize it. It's too dark. What mountain is that? There's a cornice of snow along the top ridge. The wind is blowing and there is a hazy lifting of snow whispering all along the ridge.

And now, a woman with long brown hair is crying in your arms. You can't see her face. It's as if this crying was a long time coming. She was holding back her grief for a long period of time. She feels safe enough to let it go while she is with you. Are you lovers? Why can't you see her face? Is she crying for you? Such sorrow!! It's horrible! And all you can do is hold her. What's going on?

You sit up in bed in a sweat. The sheets around you are wet. You stagger to the bathroom in the dark and turn on the hot water, pull the knob with a clunk and redirect the water up to the showerhead. As the room slowly fills with steam, you sit down on the toilet to pee. Then you sit in the tub under stream of hot rivulets. The shower curtain is pulled and the bathroom is nearly dark. You don't usually remember dreams this clearly.

You remember the feel of the rope in your hands. The tugging jangling weight of the pitons on your hip. And the feel of rock. You weren't leading. You were somewhere in the middle. A lake, far below. A sapphire lake surrounded by a thin strip of sand surrounded by an ocean of pine. And then something goes wrong.

You sit up in bed in a sweat. The sheets around you are wet. There's a woman crying, beside you. Her hair smells like lemons. It looks as if it's been bleached by the sun. There are streaks of cinnamon and straw. It's messy. Is she your lover? You lie down beside her and she puts her head on your shoulder. Her breasts press against your body. She's very sad about something. She begins to tell you but she can't talk about it. It's too painful. She leans over and turns out the light beside the bed. Dim swatches of light on the wall, and floor. This woman gets out of bed and begins to dance. You begin to know her sadness. You begin to understand her grief. You see only quick segments of her body as she dances through pools of light. A thigh. A streak of hair. Forearm. A neck. A belly. A sporadic blur of skin.

You sit up in bed in a sweat. Perhaps you've been dreaming about a woman who is very sad. You've been trying to comfort her but she holds her grief very tightly and very well. You can't get in. You're making love with her in your dream. She's on top. Is she crying? Can you feel the tickling ends of her hair across your face. Wetness. Warm water. Is she crying?

You sit up in your bed in a sweat. The cat is at the door. He's meowing to get out. Perhaps he's hungry.

"Smyth is still holding out for more money," you say. "Like he scored enough goals last season to demand anything."

What a frightening place, you think. Hospital beds lined against a dull wall. Clear bags of liquid hanging flaccid from cold steel brackets. A blue machine with lights that beep occasionally. The nurses are nice though. Pleasant and warm. Offers of blankets. Someone brings juice and cookies around too. This is your third morning. You've come to sit with your father as he takes his chemotherapy treatments.

"He's a good solid player who doesn't make many mistakes but I don't think Sather will budge," your father says.

"Sather won't crumble on this one?"

"Sather's got a budget."

"So you think Sather will let Smyth dangle?"

"It's all part of the game. Sather knows what he's doing. Best damned general manager in the business."

You always start by talking about hockey. There are certain fixed, and guaranteed entrance points to conversations between men. For you and your father, hockey was an easy door. You do not ask your father how he's doing. You simply acknowledge these procedures are necessary and also that if he was doing really well, he wouldn't be here. There's a logic and an economy of words between men.

He does not smile. Your father has stopped smiling.

It seems so long ago since you saw him smile. The absence of his smile is so profound that you remember it well. They used to occur half a face at a time. One side of his face would lift and then micro seconds later, the other side would join in. It was a crooked delay.

Just after he announced to the family he had cancer, he left a message on your answering machine: "Best that this is on the machine," he'd said. "I have something to say to you. Advice sort of. Listen, if you can, develop the ability to *know* when you're happy. When you recognize that you are happy, hang on to it as tightly as you can. Cherish it." Then there was a long pause. "I was just thinking about my life. I've been blessed with long periods of happi…" At that point the recording was cut off. You never checked with your sisters to see if they got the same message. They never said anything. Odd, to hear your father talking about the nuances of happiness.

Your father was an advertising executive with Nosko & Blanche, a small player in Edmonton but with offices and connections world-wide. He travelled a lot and always had a story about an airport, or a horror story about an airplane. Things that go bump in the flight, he used to say. Regardless, flying never seemed to bother him that much.

About ten years ago, he announced that he was moving to Hawaii to be with another woman. He'd file for divorce from there. You and your sisters were grown up already. Only your youngest sister was still at home. Your mother was not devastated. Or at least she never showed any signs of devastation. She held her head high and let him walk away. "Twenty-seven years is a good long time," she'd said. "I hope he's happy." She got on with her life. In a year, they were friendly. Called each other at Christmas and on birthdays. When his new wife, a beautiful 35-year-old Hawaiian woman named May, died giving birth, your father came back to Canada. You assume he was very happy for those two years. You assume that was what he was talking about on your machine.

Was he a good father? Do you know the difference between right and wrong? Sure you do. Well, you choose to ignore the fact you're entangled in an adultery. She's separated from her husband, you tell yourself. That's beautiful. Rationalize. Rationalize away the fact you're committing adultery. You know where she's going. She's told you. They'll be in the same house, raising their kids.

Okay, don't think about what you're doing. Basically, you're a good person. Reasonably responsible. Moderately trustworthy. A good friend. You have to blame some of your better qualities on your father, and your mother.

Even when he was following the path of his life in Hawaii you had the steady understanding that your father was on your team, no matter what. His was a quiet pride, translated through your mother and then through May's letters. There was never a face-to-face admission.

How will you cope with this if it goes badly? No, you tell yourself. Don't think like that. Remember Victoria who said: "energy follows thought", repeated it like a mantra. That was a hard concept for you to grasp but you were at least willing to try.

"You mean if I think really hard about something I can make it happen?"

"Sort of," Victoria said. "It's more like we draw certain things into our lives by dwelling on them. We put out negative energy and negative energy is drawn towards us. Bad things happen. Energy follows thought."

Booga-booga, you remember thinking. Airy-fairy, booga-booga. But you're not so sure these days. You know you don't like being around negative people. You're drawn, without rational thought, towards positive people.

"Look at this modern-day torture chamber," your father says. "You have to have hope or you wouldn't do this."

"Me? I should have hope? I do have hope," you say stupidly.

"No, no, I'm talking about me."

"Ya, I know this is an act of hope. I know that. I also know that you're going to be fine." You think about the dogged determination and strength it takes to go through with this and not crack. It would be easy to crumble.

"This is not much fun but I'll get through it. Listen, we'll have to buy a couple golds for a game when I'm through this."

"I only come down here to give you some sort of comic relief. I'm afraid I haven't been very goddamned funny."

He nods his head. A fragile gesture somehow. It's as if he has gone back to being a new-born baby with wobbly, unsure neck muscles.

"And, you know, I figured you could use the company," you add.

A long silence. A nurse walks by. Her shoes don't match. Your father looks off into the corner. He looks back at you with a small shift of knowledge, a new light, a knowing light, in his eyes. It's as if something wonderful has just dawned on him.

"I really appreciate you being here," he says. And he offers a small smile.

You don't say anything. A machine beeps like a truck backing up. A nurse stops the beeping and changes a bag of clear fluid. A woman in the corner goes into the bathroom and doesn't come out for a long time.

"So you think Sather will hold his ground on Smyth?"

"Yes," your father says. "Yes, I do."

"Z?" Frannie says. The expression on her face is hard to read.

"Ya, it's a, well, it's a long story."

"I've got time," she says.

You can't tell if she's irritated, or amused.

"A while back I dated a woman with a lot of tattoos and she wanted me to get one too. So, I've got this more-or-less permanent record of our time together on my ass. It hurt like a son-of-a-bitch."

"And exactly what does it represent?"

You know it's a stylized 'N'. Why not just tell her it stands for Noreen? It's not as if they'll ever meet. Or at least the chances of that are very small.

"It's her initial."

"What's her name? Zora? Zelda?"

"No."

"Zena? Zoe?"

"No, you have to tilt your head."

"That's not an 'H' is it?" Something hard in her voice. She's threatened by this. She's threatened by Hannah. Why? Well, maybe she should feel threatened. You're writing and sending poems to this woman across the country. You've told her about Hannah. Not everything. Not your campaign of poetry. You thought it was only fair to share part of your recent history. You have not told Frannie that if Hannah phoned you and said *come*, you'd have a problem. If Hannah wrote and said *I need you*, you might be in trouble.

You roll over on your back.

"No. It's not an 'H'."

Frannie can probably hear the dullness in your voice. Your words seem to drop on the floor like dead fish. She decides it's best to back off on this one.

"I kinda like it," she says. And you believe she really does like it.

"Good God. Has the world gone completely tattoo crazy? You don't want me to get one too, do you?"

"Could we change this one into an 'F'?"

Our possessions are the source of our pain.

The Italian writer Italo Calvino once wrote: 'One is what one does not throw away.'

Define love. Please.

The things we hang on to help define us. Is that what Calvino means? And you are hanging on to Hannah. So you are Hannah. Because you will not throw her away, you are her.

You dream that your imaginary nun, Domonique, is making love. She is in a meadow, naked on a blanket. The sky is moving too fast. The clouds are flying by as if the entire world, except here on this blanket, was moving at double time. The tree-tops move in real time and then slow down. They sway in a drunken dance, staggered in time. She's having her period but that does not matter. Now is a good time to make love and feel some sense of security about not becoming pregnant. It's important that she not become pregnant. That can't happen. Not now. Not with this man. She loves this man but not that way. She's been down that road before. In her dream, she has had children. The kisses. Their kisses are a perfect delight.

But this can't be me, she thinks. I do not have children. This is not me.

When they are finally lying on their sides, breathing each other, exhausted, Domonique knows that she's pregnant. She knows this woman is pregnant. It's not her. It's someone else.

And then the woman who has been making love holds Domonique. She caresses Domonique's breasts and traces the curve of her hip—nibbles at the back of her neck. The woman does not know. She doesn't know she's pregnant. She thinks she's protected by a little blood.

When the man pulls out there is blood. There is a smear of red down the woman's inner thighs. But they are in love and driven by a lust neither of them understands. The act is all. The kiss. The penetration. The need. The orgasm. The touch. The desire. The risk of conception. And then again…the touch. The desire. The penetration. The kiss. The need. The orgasm. The risk…

Domonique stands up. She's naked. There is blood smudged down her thighs. She looks across the clearing at three deer. There are coyotes howling at the edge of things. The deer move closer without fear. Large, innocent eyes. Radar ears. Softness. There is no bird song.

Domonique looks at the woman and the man, sleeping now. Domonique needs to decipher who they are. She has to know. But their faces are blurred. "Who are you?" she wants to scream but her mouth is dry, her throat a desert. The woman has a small trickle of blood pooling on the blanket beneath her crotch. There's too much blood, Domonique thinks. She moves to the woman's side and touches her shoulder, trying to get her attention. The woman moans at her touch, writhes a little. Starts to become sexual. You're bleeding, Domonique wants to say. You're bleeding a lot.

⊱⊷⊰

You remember your dream in the shower. Domonique's face was almost Hannah's. You saw glimpses of her face. You wonder if you should maybe try to call Hannah, to see if she's alright. Illogical. Think about that conversation: Listen, I had this dream where you bled a lot. And I was, well, I needed to know you were all right.

You reach outside the shower curtain for your coffee. As you bring the mug into the shower you bump your elbow and spill half your coffee into the tub. It mixes dark with the water, is diluted and quickly swirls down the drain.

⊱⊷⊰

Somewhere in the *I Ching* it says: *work on what is already ruined.* What is ruined in you? Your capacity for normal is altered by this experience. How do you go into a relationship that promises to press on and on into the future? And with each passing month and year a history masses up behind. And perhaps it will degrade into mediocrity or the permafrost of complacency. How can you accept all this when you know about life and death suspended in a single flutter of a sparrow's wing, the beginning and the ending held in a single breath?

What about new loves, new connections? Will you and Hannah and Norm always be looking over your shoulders? Will the potential for infidelity always be on the surface of your lives? Have you become a trinity of faithless doubters?

Will each new relationship you three march into be painted with this skeptical colour? A butterfly flaps its wings in Japan and a day later there's a hurricane in Florida. A woman kisses a man in the trunk of his car in Edmonton and a year later a man on the other side of the country is unable to trust anybody or anything, least of all his wife.

Perhaps, you think, it is possible to grow trust. Perhaps we can learn to trust all over again. If that is the case, you ought to find out who sells the seed and send away for a package. Spring is coming. You could start them inside while winter rages on the other side of the balcony windows of your apartment. Snow could drift listlessly past your window and inside you would be tending those tiny seeds, misting the soil, praying for germination. You imagine the seeds as small and brown, like lobelia seeds. And if you're successful, you could send other packages to friends. It would be like braided sweet-grass. You would never sell it. It would only be for giving away freely with an open heart, with respect and humility.

Roughly four years ago, a group of six climbers stops just above what they call the Big Step on the east ridge of Cavell.

"There're a couple interesting pitches above here," Bob says.

Michelle looks up, nods her head, says: "The snow worries me."

They both look at the snow. They've been on it for the last hour. It's a heavy, wet snow that packs well. They do not know what's under it.

None of them have been on this mountain before. The other four are huddled around a burner, waiting for tea, munching on energy bars.

"*Festina lente,*" Bob says. He looks at Michelle. An irrefutable blond bombshell. She's the type of woman I'd never stand a chance with, he thinks. I'd be afraid to approach her for a date because she's too damned striking. It's a good thing we're friends.

"What?"

"It's Latin. It means to hurry slowly. That's what we should be doing. Well, perhaps *hurry carefully* would be better." It was Franz who taught Bob this phrase. Franz taught Bob everything he knew about climbing. Whenever Bob was in trouble on a rock face, he'd hear Franz's steady voice from above, or below: *festina lente, festina lente.* Franz had had a glorious climbing career until something went wrong on K2. Best to not even think about it while on a mountain, any mountain. He looks over at the other four. A woman from that group brings him a cup of tea. She has hair the colour of rich loamy earth. “Thank you,” he says to her and then winks lovingly. She sneers at him. It’s as if she has brought him the tea out of a deep-seated love but she’s bloody pissed off at him right now. It is not that she’s jealous of his quiet discussions with Michelle. It’s something else. An argument before the climb, or a small disagreement about something stupid.

Michelle is looking at the sky. “If we get a hot day, this snow could ice up right under our feet in the afternoon.”

“I know,” Bob says. “The problem is, I can’t tell how much old snow is underneath this new stuff. We’d better get our asses up this mountain.” He turns to the group. “Let’s get moving. Everyone okay?”

Bob takes the lead as they plod up the mountain. Everybody makes it through the pitches without too much trouble and with good speed. They’re all fairly experienced climbers.

Soon, they will hit the first of the false summits. Several more will follow. Bob had read about these and he is ready for them. It’s discouraging to think you’re nearly there, to know you’ve climbed well and hard and fast, and your journey to the summit is almost over only to have it taken away by another higher summit which will in turn be replaced by an even higher summit. Eventually, climbers become sneering cynics when they look up and see what appears to be the top.

six

Becoming Human

It was the first time in the history of the park that the Parks Administration were attempting to keep the hot springs open all year. The hot springs could easily handle any weather. The road was the problem. It wound itself through elevation gains and losses, and one absolutely unreasonable hair-pin turn. If the road iced up, even a little, it became a menacing snake. The shoulders, for the most part, were cliffs into the valley.

It was only fifteen kilometres from the main highway to the springs but to keep it open and safe was going to be a challenge. With a new airport in Hinton up and running, there would be more tourists wanting to experience the hottest natural hot springs in the Rocky Mountains.

"I think there will not be too much business this first winter," Nick says. "But the next year—once word gets around—will be good. So, we will have a relaxing few months." He smiles at the ceiling of their room and Marta moves herself closer to her husband. It's cold this morning, she's thinking. She would have to bring out the thick eider-down quilt tomorrow.

"The heating system for the motel is cranky but all right. I'm worried a little about the cabins." Nick rolls over. Moves his hand down the line of Marta's hip and buttock. The feel of her skin is a delight. It is still a delight after all these years.

They have been moving back and forth from the resort to the town-site for a decade. Nick split his time between the hot springs resort and the Chickadee restaurant in town. It was only an hour drive. He had a cousin in Vancouver who commuted four hours back and forth from work every day. And that was when the traffic was good.

Nick's commute was infrequent, with scattered traffic, and with staggeringly beautiful mountains for scenery. He had never once complained about the drive in the twelve years. He felt blessed.

He decides that ordering extra firewood for the cabins would be a good idea. The little fireplaces would be a necessity this winter. Between the fireplaces and the small electrical heaters, and extra blankets they would be fine.

You find out about the new policy on your way home. It's usually the last weekend the springs are open. You decided you could use a good soaking in the springs after Fitzwilliam and of course, Frannie is there. You're not sure what you want to do with her. Nothing. You just want to see her. If you can see her, it proves everything else is real.

There, in the front entrance, is a brochure explaining the pool will not close this year as part of a three-year pilot project.

Our tax dollars at work. Here's something you can support.

You take Jean Vanier's *Becoming Human* with you into the pool. You like to read while you soak. It's not the kind of book you would normally buy. But you heard the author on the radio delivering a series of lectures which would eventually become this book. At the time, your father had just announced he was sick. You were occupied with thoughts of your father. You did not want to listen to a lecture on becoming human. But you could not help but listen to it. You were driving home to your apartment on a cool fall night. Cool enough for a thick wool sweater, leather gloves, a scarf. You were thinking about death. You had not started to be optimistic about anything. In the first minute, Vanier had you. You would have liked to have shut off the car radio and run inside your apartment to finish listening but you really did not want to miss one word. Here was this man pleading for human beings to become more human. To treat each other with respect and kindness. And how do we discover our humanness? Through mutual dependency, through weakness, by learning through belonging. We do not become human by being alone, he said. It's through belonging.

So you listened to the remaining lecture in the car and the following three nights, you set time aside to listen. And now, the book. You settle back with your head on the edge of the pool and read.

(25)
pale saint grace

the snow follows her intention
an even, white surface through the night
—blows in hours before she turns the key
slips her cool body beside you
begins to look for the places
gently, with insignificant hands
She creates a delicate sanctuary
tactile waves of pleasure
Together, you dreamily surrender
drift in a middle-of-the-night loving
both frantic and kind
Finally, tangled in each other
you sleep peaceful as nuns
In the morning, there is steaming coffee
on the bedside table

—the cool after-snow scent
through the screened window
—the sound of dripping water
And she is gone
She takes you into her day
leaves only melting foot steps
—evenly spaced hollows in the snow
under gray stick trees
a requiem of cloud
and the pale twinkling songs
of bewildered chickadees.

Is there some safe place for you to rest and line up these events in order—make sense of everything that's happened? At the end of this story perhaps? But where is that, you're asking yourself. Where is the end of this story? Have you gone past the end?

What about the order? Why can't you remember this in order? Do you have a narrative dyslexia? Is this some sort of raw avoidance tactic?

Okay. It was in the spring. You met Hannah in the spring. And then in July you started to write poems. Was it four months? In July, she was gone. And in the spring, a year later, Frannie called you during the Oilers' first play-off game. Has a year gone by already? And your father died. Noreen knows about wine. And you began writing poetry. Noreen knows a lot about sex. Where is the cat? She's an expert on sex. Fifty-two poems. One every week for a year. And then what? It wasn't Hannah calling you was it? How in the hell did Frannie get so impossibly caught up in this narrative?

It's ludicrous. You can only hope that at some point in the future there will be a room in which you can sit. A room with a fig tree against a bag-of-oranges wall where you can sit in an armchair and ruminate. And there will be someone who cares about your soul. They'll guard you. Protect your loneliness. Not ask a million stupid questions. Let you unfold if you wish. Or stay closed if that is your need. They will feed your body, hold you closely in the night, and allow you to heal.

And there will be a cat. A gray cat who will sense something is wrong and offer comfort the way only cats can. She will curl against your body while you sleep. She will need to be fed. She will need to be loved and petted. She will need to go outside and to come back inside. She will need to be brushed. And you will do all this without once ever thinking it is a chore.

And what about the 52nd poem? Hannah would never know. She couldn't possibly know you never sent it. You didn't write it so you couldn't bloody well send it could you? Why would you tell Hannah? She doesn't need to know.

You do not finish what you started. That's not like you.

seven

the elk pasture

She's not there. Frannie's not there. She's working a wedding in Jasper. She'll be back on Tuesday. You won't be here that long. You'll come back in a few weeks, you decide. Marta tells you this. She supplies information with an even, ingenuous lack of prejudice. If she knows something, she tells it.

"That one is in Jasper," she says. "A wedding. Her next shift is Wednesday morning. You can leave a message for her if you like."

Ha. That's funny. You haven't even met Frannie yet, officially. You leave Marta at the counter and go into the restaurant for a cup of coffee. When you sit down at the table, you're already drifting. It's just a quick release on your part. An image comes inside a shrug of your shoulders. It's that quick. You imagine Frannie and you walking down a street in a small town. It's not Jasper, although, there are mountains. Apparently, you've had babies. There are two small children with you. Frannie's got her hair in a ponytail. The sky is narrow and blue. You're incredibly happy.

Well, wasn't that completely irrational and stupid. Your daydream makes you smile. You look over at Marta and wonder if she's happy.

Does she still love her husband? Does she long for the city? Perhaps this is not the life she'd have chosen. Did she imagine that she'd be living in a place where one had to watch for bears and mountain lions when she first met Nick? A life where the damned sheep ravage her flowers every time she turns her back. A place where a month without snow was a rare event.

Growing up in a tourist town probably wasn't the best environment for girls but they'd turned out just fine. One daughter manages the Chickadee in town, the other is in university in Calgary, studying anthropology.

You find out about Marta and Nick's kids, about the weather in the mountains, by nodding at a picture on the wall beside the cash register. The picture is of the two daughters and Nick at the summit of a mountain with snow falling around them.

"Your daughters?" you say, and then Marta is off. Perhaps, she is not so friendly and outgoing with everyone.

(29)

In the pool, The Elk Pasture hot springs

This morning the clouds nest in the valley

Up at the pool, rising steam and descending cloud
create a messy meeting of white

This murky barrier hides Mount Shuey behind,
Sulphur Ridge to the left
and a high coral shelf to the right

Even without hard proof
I know these mountains exist

The two old German women
beside me in the pool
have no memory to draw upon

They have never climbed or hiked these peaks

They have no tactile experience

"Have you been here before?" I say
They look confused
Hesitantly, unsure— "We are our first time in Canada."
"Up there," I point, "is a mountain with a coral reef for a ridge.
It was pushed up a long time ago. Used to be the bottom of the ocean."
I draw a line with my hands, like I'm petting an elephant
They look confused
"Oh," they say finally
Although nothing ever sounds soft in German,
the women speak softly to each other
They are likely discussing the lunatic next to them—
a man who believes there's an ocean
at the top of a mountain that they can't see
A mountain they will not see today
A mountain they will likely never see

In the morning, Nick is smoking a cigar and reading a newspaper on the deck outside the restaurant. You sit down beside him and say nothing. When he looks up over the newspaper, he smiles. A kindness from his eyes.

"Good. Good you're here." Then a concern across his face. "You alone?"

"She's gone," you say and Nick just nods.

"You need coffee."

A waitress appears as if on cue.

"Two more of these," Nick says. He points at an empty coffee cup. He folds the newspaper on to the table and looks at you. "How have you been?"

My father is dying, you want to say. This was something you could talk about with certainty. It put everything else into perspective. “My father’s fighting cancer. He’s a battler. He’ll make it through all right.”

You might think the shadow of death would distract you from thoughts about Hannah but it doesn’t. You’d like to tell Nick how much you miss her. How you have a yearning that you don’t understand. Here, at least, is someone who saw you two together.

“I’m sorry to hear that.”

“The treatments are going well. They say they caught it quite early.”

The coffee arrives. You notice the waitress smells; a faint hint of under-arm odour. You can’t help noticing these things. She delivers the coffee, carefully places the cups in saucers on the table, and leaves quickly.

“I thought you were only in Jasper,” you say. “I didn’t know, I didn’t expect to see you…”

“… My wife and I run both places. My brother helps too but mostly he likes to bet the horses in Edmonton. So he’s not around much. He does not love the mountains. Are you here long?”

“I have to leave tomorrow.”

“Next time, perhaps you and I could do a little climbing.”

“Oh, I don’t really climb. It’s mostly scrambling and hiking. I just love being up there.”

“A small hike then.”

“It’s a deal. Perhaps in a couple weeks.”

You sit together and talk about different hikes and trails you’ve been on. The blond waitress with the faint odour brings coffee at regular intervals. The sun is soft. It seems to take its time getting hot. There’s a cool breeze blowing down from Sulphur Ridge so you don’t really notice it. Nick does not ask you what happened between you and Hannah.

When you call home there is a message on your machine from your mother. “He’s gone. Your father had a heart attack this morning,” she says. “It was fast. He didn’t suffer.” And then silence.

Fuck.

You phone your mother. Your sister, Susan, answers.

"Where are you?"

"I'm at the Elk Pasture. I just heard. I'll be home tomorrow." You're standing outside the main office. It's the only public phone at the lodge. Hold it together, you tell yourself. Hold everything together until later. Freeze whatever liquid there is in you until later.

"Good," she says.

Melody wouldn't have been able to have this conversation without sobbing. Her emotions were always lurking close to the surface. Susan was more like you; a wild undertow.

"What the hell happened?"

"He just had a heart attack. A massive heart attack."

Silence.

"How are you holding up? How's mom doing?"

More silence.

"Oh, you know. She's a trooper. But we're all in shock. We need you here."

"I'll see you tomorrow."

"We'll look for you. Drive carefully okay?"

"See you tomorrow."

"Love you."

Back in your room, you begin to fill the hip flask with scotch, holding it above the sink. You're not steady enough to do this so instead slip the whole bottle into the inner pocket of your coat. Outside the room, you do not know where you're going. You begin to walk up towards the pool. But find yourself sitting on a picnic table beside the road. Three big horn sheep across the road are pulling at the grass. One of them looks up at you and it reminds you of a cat you used to have.

Someone has punched you in the face very hard. You have the swelling, throbbing feeling in your head. You see perfectly fine but you're off balance. Or did you step on a rake. And the handle came up suddenly and whacked you in the middle of your face. You can feel the blood pumping under your skin.

Someone is standing in front of you. Your father's doing all right. He's a battler. He's going to make it through this. Jesus, he's gone. What was the last thing you said? What was your last conversation? Were you kind to each other? You can't recall what you said last. That's it. He's gone. There's someone standing in front of you. There's someone…

"What's wrong?"

"Nothing," you say. Who the fuck wants to know, you think.

"Are you all right?"

It's Nick for Christ's sake. There's a wheel barrow abandoned behind him, a shovel on the ground. Look at his face. He's really worried. You must look like shit.

"Ah, my dad…My dad…He died this morning." A flat statement. Even you notice your voice is without life. "While I was in the hot springs, my dad died. A heart attack."

While you were enjoying yourself, your dad died. You never said good-bye. You thought he was all right. You thought he was going to make it. Why the fuck would you say that kind of good-bye?

"I'm sorry," Nick says.

He looks as shocked as you feel. And concerned. Perhaps he's had his own losses. No, he's definitely had his own losses, you decide. He knows you right now because he has been you.

"Listen, if you want to talk," Nick says. "I'll buy you a drink. I'm in the bar." He takes a few steps toward the wheelbarrow, picks up the shovel. Then he turns around. "Come. Even if you don't feel like talking."

(37)

untitled

I cannot cry
even in the humid, cradled arms
of sunless winter
my eyes are a desert

So cauterize this snow
let this pathetic gray ceiling oppress
because I cannot tear
It's as if I expect to see you tomorrow
at kitchen table with coffee and your crooked smile
As if I will talk with you in the comfortable place
that was between us
"Why hello," you will say, "Why don't you cry? It's normal you know."
and I will smile: "But I have always been terrified of normal."
"So that was it," you'll say, nodding your gray head.
"And whom shall I cry for?"
"We weep for ourselves," you'll say.
"Can you help me to let go of this?"
"You have no choice. You're hanging on to nothing."
"But something in me is clinging."
you'll pause and look evenly at me, say: "Be alone for a while.
listen to wolves at dusk. You'll know what to do."

Stop these words which are dark stand-ins for tears
close this journal of scribbled disorganizations
tie on boots and pull on sweater, jacket, and move,
move outside into the squeaking chaotic snow,
under an injured sky

In the mountains, listen

Walk until spring warms these shifting bones
and the glare off the snow squints my face,
splays wrinkles at eyes' corners,
and so many new things are born
and it all begins again.

When you drift into the restaurant there is a bottle of cognac on the table, and two snifters. Nick's reading a hard-cover book. He stands up as you come in. He picks up the bottle and the glasses and says "come."

You sit on the deck, hidden at a corner table. Nick pours from the crystal bottle and you sit quietly for a while. It's cool but you are both wearing sweaters. You notice someone has left thick woolen blankets on a bench next to the building.

"Apparently there are two mountain lions up at the old springs," Nick says. "One of the pool attendants spotted them last night. They've taken four sheep already. Perhaps more. Hard to tell. There are a lot of sheep in this herd."

You sniff the cognac. The heady aroma travels through your head and down your throat. It gives you the illusion of clear-headedness. You take a big sip of the cognac. It seems to disappear in a smoky, earthy mist in your mouth before you get a chance to swallow.

Nick continues to tell you about the mountain lions. "Wardens have been up to move the kills. Too close to the water source for the pool. They were worried about bacteria. That's got to piss off a mountain lion, having his food moved."

"Yes, I wouldn't be too happy about that." You imagine sitting down at your favorite restaurant for a schnitzel and half way through your meal, maybe when you get up to go to the bathroom, the waitress comes and moves your plate to a different table.

"The sheep. The herd was getting too large. The mountain lions show up and presto, it's back to a healthy size. The lions do the work of nature. Life and death, you know? And life goes on now." Nick pours more cognac into your glass. He pulls two cigars out of his jacket pocket.

"That goddamned ewe that eats Marta's flowers survived. I've noticed she's hanging around the lodge a lot more these days. Smart lady, that one. Marta would love to see that sheep go for a long walk by the old hot springs."

Nick stops talking. He knows he's been blathering. Still, after six decades of life, the right words just do not come. He doesn't know what to say except to fill up the air with a gentle wall of words. Perhaps a wall for you to lean on. He looks down at the cigars which he's placed on the table.

"Do you smoke?"

"No. It's a little too *in fashion* for my liking."

"Fashion? Forget fashion. You should try it. Nothing slows you down like a good cigar. Even a not-so-good cigar will slow you down. Nothing is rushed when you smoke a cigar. The world slows." He looks at you. Picks up a cigar, holds it between his thumb and four fingers. Rolls it slightly with his thumb. "No time like the present."

Nick begins to teach you about cigars. The ritual surrounding the smoking of a cigar, for Nick, is equivalent to the ceremony surrounding a high mass. You've never seen anything so seemingly banal become almost holy.

"This is a Churchill," he says. "From the Dominican Republic. Not a particularly good Churchill but it has a gentle flavour. It's a good place to start."

It takes ten minutes to light them and then you find you actually enjoy the flavour the smoke leaves in your mouth. At about the half way point of your smoke, Marta walks out and looks at the two of you, frowns, and walks back inside.

"Marta doesn't approve?"

"She's only worried about me," Nick says. "I had problem with…a small problem with my health a couple years ago. I'm not supposed to smoke. I don't smoke as much as I used to."

You sit silently with Nick for a long time after that. He didn't mean to remind you. He tried not to remind you. You try to think about the pines, the sky, the heavenly taste of the cognac, the fact you're smoking a cigar. But you can only think of your father. You are there with your father. You are immersed in your illogical guilt. You are already with your mother and sisters. You are in the future without your father.

After a long silence, Nick pours more cognac. Then he reaches across the table and grabs your wrist with his hand and squeezes a little. “I’m very sorry about your father,” he says. Then he leans back against the wall and is silent.

In the morning when you go to pay your bill, you find you don’t have one. Marta looks at you with soft eyes and says quite firmly that it’s been taken care of. You would normally protest but this morning you just nod and say thank you. As you head for the door, you almost bump into Nick who is carrying a mug of steaming coffee, which he presses into your hand.

“Safe journey,” he says.

“Thank you. The mug. I…”

“…you’ll bring it back with you the next time you come.” He smiles. You notice for the first time that Nick is missing a tooth in the upper left corner of his mouth.

She calls back just before the end of the second period.

Who calls back? Who the hell is calling you during the hockey game? Well, who do you think? The one with whom you share damage. Boy you really know how to not pick ’em. Well you don’t really pick ’em do you? You’ve spent the first half of your life trying to develop a sense of self-esteem that doesn’t suck. You look around at what’s in front of you and you become curious. You don’t chase women, you just appear to be romantic and charming. Women come sniffing around to see what the hell you’re about and you try to hook the ones who seem interesting. Hannah, for instance, had to kiss you. She kissed you as you stood behind the car. Then like a good fisherwoman she hooked you into her life. She pulled you into her life, flopping and floundering.

Does anybody get through life undamaged in some way? Does anybody ever get through a relationship without taking a hit? It’s ludicrous for you to think you’re special.

The Oilers are down by a goal but they seem to have the momentum. They’re hitting everything that moves and skating their hearts out. They are not as talented as the other team but Jesus they want to win. You think about your dad. He’d have loved this. Smyth settled on Sather’s terms, just as your father predicted, and he is playing like a mad person. He'd showed up two weeks into the season ready to go.

When the phone rings, you know it's her.

You pick it up and say hello.

"Hi," Noreen says. "I just thought I'd call you and see how you've been."

"Noreen?"

"So," she says, pushing at the edge of your awkwardness, "how have you been?"

She expects you to say *horrible*, you think, or *not so great*. That it's been awful without her in your life. That you're lonely. That you miss her. That you made a mistake in stopping the relationship. That she was the best thing that ever happened to you.

"I'm good," you say.

"Hey, that's great."

"And you?"

"I miss you. I…"

"…Noreen, don't."

"I know, but…"

"…Don't."

"All right, all right. But do you know what I've got on?"

You are silent. You think about the obscenely large collection of lingerie, about the toys. All these things flash through your mind.

"Let's not start this conversation again."

"I know, but I need you. I need you tonight. Come over and make love and then you can go. I won't bug you. You don't have to sleep with me. Just come over. Or I can come over there. I won't stay long."

"How much booze have you had?"

"Champagne. Lots of Champagne."

"Look…"

"…champagne pee is sweet and warm," she breathes. "Remember."

"Jesus, Noreen."

You've been seeing Frannie for two months, commuting back and forth from the city to the mountains, when she turns to you one night and says "I was married."

"Yes, I know," you say.

You look around the small cabin. It's the middle of winter, early February. It's a small space but very comfortable. Thick wooden beams cut across the ceiling. There's a small nook of a kitchen and an equally scaled-down bathroom. The cabin was Frannie's home until spring when the heavy tourist season would begin. Along the top of the head-board are a good assortment of books. It seems that with every visit you add to the row. You might bring a book you love, or one that Frannie asked you to pick up. With no television except down in the dining room, reading becomes a graceful replacement. Across the room is a small fireplace that's almost constantly in use. Right next to the bed is an inadequate but welcome electric heater which tries hard but was only meant to take the chill out of the room in the summer months.

Frannie squats in front of the fire, pulls the stand-alone screen away and adds more wood. She's wearing only pale green long underwear. When she turns around you feel lucky, blessed. Here is this beautiful, tall, woman who cares about you. Look at her. See the way she walks across the room? Imagine you are smoothing the lush curves of one of her breasts. Feel the liquid fullness, the weight, the satin pleasure of her skin. And the way she looks at you. A possibility of every kindness. That look, her head tilted slightly, and her lifting smile make you feel loved. Can you still hold Hannah in reserve? Is it possible to love Hannah and Frannie at the same time?

"My husband died," she says.

"Yes, you told me. While climbing."

She crawls under the quilt, presses against your side, talks to your shoulder. There's something wrong here, you think. Why is she repeating this? Surely she remembers she's already told you.

"I didn't tell you everything."

Well, that gets you thinking. She killed him, you think and then: No, that's completely idiotic. But what? What else is there to tell?

When you first meet Frannie again it's a disaster. It's a month after your father passed away. The road to the resort is fine. It's been a mild, fairly dry winter so far. It's snowing now though. Big, steady flakes drift through still air. The snow falling makes you feel a bit melancholy. You don't know why. Perhaps it reminds you that life goes on. Regardless of grief, or yearning, or pain or delight, the snow will still fall. Oh stop being so fucking symbolic, you tell yourself. Snow is snow.

You and Nick are talking over breakfast about plans to go up Mount Shuey in the spring. It's a scramble at most. Light climbing at the very worst. These are winter dreams of climbing and hiking in the spring. She trundles up the steps with an over-night bag on her shoulder and a small day pack on her back. Nick makes introductions. You are sitting in one of the front window seats with your coffee. She doesn't remember you clearly. There's a glimmer of recognition but it never solidifies. So you begin again.

Nick introduces you, gives your name a slow importance.

You half stand up—like you're in some Carry Grant movie—to shake her hand. "Pleased to meet you." She gives you that half-recognition tilt to her head and then says "Hi." There are melting snow flakes scattered on her shoulders and in her hair. She's wearing one of those shearling coats that you love. The coat hangs open and falls to her knees. You imagine it's never actually been done up.

There's something cold about the look she gives you. You wonder what the hell it could be. In your memory, your interaction with her in town was fine.

Nick asks her to join you and she says she wants to drop her bags off and check on Pal first. She slips her coat off as she walks towards the kitchen doorway. Nick begins to unravel what he knows about Frannie. He doesn't tell everything he knows. Just enough to pique your interest. When she arrives at your table, Frannie's wearing blue jeans and an emerald coloured sweat shirt. She's not on duty until 6 p.m.

"How is the road?"

"It's all right except for that damned turn. I crawled the car through it. They were sanding the road coming towards me so I assume it's better now."

Nick nods.

Well, if Nick likes her, she must be quite something, you think.

"We were talking about going up Shuey," Nick says. "In the spring. Maybe you'd like to come along. We could use someone who actually knows what they're doing."

Frannie looks at Nick. "You haven't told him about your exploits?"

"Oh, I don't talk much about that anymore," Nick says.

"And I don't climb anymore," she says. There's a tired bitterness just under the surface of this statement. She says it quickly, with a jagged edge.

"Well, it's just a hike really," Nick says. " We won't even need rope."

"I don't climb at all."

You join Nick in his persuasion. "Maybe you'll change your mind in the spring?"

"No," she says. "I won't, so just fucking drop it, okay." Frannie gets up. "I'm sorry. I have to get ready for work."

"I…" you say.

"Thanks for the coffee." Then she's gone, weaving her way through tables towards the door.

When Frannie's coffee arrives at the table, she's long since gone. You're stunned by her departure. You sit and look at the snow drifting past the restaurant window. What the hell was that about?

"It's her husband," Nick says finally. "An accident."

"God, me and my big bloody mouth."

"I thought that pain was further down than it is. My mistake for allowing the conversation to go that way. Not your fault. You could not have known."

Cavell's summit ridge is completely covered with snow. They have to slow down to a crawl. At one point they cut steps with an axe. The sun sneaks out from behind clouds and it begins to get very hot. Sunglasses come out of packs and pockets. Fleece jackets come off. They press on to the top and reach it in good time. There is a steel cross at the summit. They celebrate with tea in the bright sunlight made brighter by the snow's albedo.

Six-and-half hours to the summit is good time, Bob thinks.

Just before the summit, the snow had given way under their weight causing some anxious moments along a corniced ridge. Bob had almost stopped the team and roped up but with careful movements and ice picks they'd managed to slog through to the top.

This time, Bob takes tea to her. She takes the tea and says a curt thank you. He reaches out to give her a hug and her body stiffens.

"I love you, lady," he whispers. "More than I can say."

"What? The horses need some hay?"

"You heard me," he says.

We'll sort it out later, he thinks. Right now, she's angry. Give her space. Let her enjoy this view.

"Problems?" Michelle says quietly.

"Nothing that can't be sorted out."

He pulls a small camera from his pack and snaps a quick picture of the summit and the small group of climbers.

"That's what I like about you two."

"What?"

"You always manage to work things out. I mean, how many times have you almost crashed? And to everybody around you, it's blatantly obvious that you love each other."

Bob holds up his cup of tea. He looks around him at a panorama of peaks and sky. He never tires of being at the top of things. Then he looks at his climbing partners. "To old Edith Cavell," he says. He pulls out a small journal and reads: "Climbing the mountain is not enough. We must have no hatred or bitterness for anyone."

"To Edith," they mutter, then raise their own mugs and drink.

"Bitterness? Hatred?" Michelle looks at him.

"An Edith Cavell quote. It's on her statue in London."

They'd all read the plaque in the parking lot. "Edith Cavell, the nurse," Michelle says. "She was a climber?"

"Actually, I think she said 'Patriotism is not enough' but I really don't think she'd have minded. She lived her life on the edge. At least the last part, up until she was shot by the Germans."

After resting, they decide to descend quickly by the *Normal Route* in order to make a round trip of it. They approach another ridge of corniced snow with cheerful hearts. Someone shouts back that they've hidden two six-packs of beer under a rock in the lake, which is only a small gem below.

You find the club in an out-of-the-way strip mall, in the west end of the city. You'd stopped for gas on the way out of town and happened to see the sign across the road. Gentlemen's Club, it said. And so you find yourself sitting inside a strip bar, in a strip mall—you find this to be quite funny—drinking a beer and watching a tall blond woman in high heels dancing naked on stage. It's not the first time you've been in a strip bar but you're certainly not a frequent flyer.

The woman on stage has strange patterns of lightened skin all up her buttocks crack and around the front. Like someone placed leaves on her skin before she tanned. Perhaps she painted those patterns on with some sort of sunscreen and then crawled into a tanning booth, you think. And she would have had to do it more than once. What a high maintenance job. But the effect of her tanning work is absolutely stunning under the black light on stage. What the hell is it with you and patterned women?

It seems like she wants to talk. She's walking around the stage flirting with the guys who sit up close. Smiling and laughing, she's trying to strike up conversations above the booming music. A flop of blond hair keeps falling across her face and she pushes it back behind her ear several times. Odd that she would want to make connections in a place where it's all watching and never touching. Here was this patterned woman, trying to make connections. Fascinating. And the DJ announcer, hidden in a booth somewhere, was teasing her about it. "Men come here for two reasons," he says. "Beer and titties. They don't come here to talk." "I was just making friends," she says. "Titties and beer," he says. "But, I thought we could have an intelligent conversation," she blurts. "Titties and beer," he says over the p.a. As she's getting dressed, the announcer says: "That was the lovely Stacey. Ya, that's right gentlemen, Stacey will be back with her degree in criminology, at around ten-thirty, later tonight."

You love it when the strippers get dressed. Getting dressed, even if it's just pulling a dress on, is the sexiest, most natural thing a stripper does, to your mind. And then they walk around the stage picking up the dollar and two-dollar coins the men in wanker row have thrown on stage. When they're picking up their coins it's showtime again. But for a minuscule moment, as they dress, there is no show and that's what you find erotic.

Wouldn't it be amazing to actually have conversations with strippers while they were dancing? A strip bar where the women came out and stripped but then talked about philosophy, or English, or maybe read poetry while they were removing their clothes. That would be something. They engage your crotch and your head at the same time. That would be dangerous. With libido and intellect engaged, it's just a baby step to the heart.

You don't finish your beer. It was just a prop. You've got a long drive ahead. As Stacey walks by your seat, on her way out the door, you get a small whiff of a dark, earthy perfume. Something like an after-rain scent. You'd love to come back and see more of her but you'll be on the road by then, on your way to see Frannie. And Nick.

"We got off to a bad start," you say to Frannie.

"No, I got off to a bad start. I'm sorry. I'm a little sensitive about climbing. It's my history. It's my fault."

"Nick told me a bit of the story. But I think he's protective of people he likes. Someday, maybe, when you feel like it, I'd like to hear what happened."

"Yes. Nick is romantic that way."

You're sitting at the bar, slightly off to the side, in the dining room. Frannie's drinking a bottle of beer, from the bottle. You order a scotch in hopes of sparking a memory. The sound of a dishwasher running comes from behind a set of swinging doors. And then she just starts talking.

"He was on Edith Cavell, the East Ridge. The team reached the summit and they were on their way down..."

You want to ask questions but you also don't want to interrupt.

"Six. There were six altogether. All experienced climbers. The East Ridge is not a difficult climb. It's spectacular but it's not overly difficult. Anyway, a cornice...do you know what a cornice is?"

You nod.

"Well, a cornice broke away and took him and two others. No one survived. It was 200 metres almost straight down. I know one of the women that made it down. We still keep in touch."

"I'm sorry for your loss." What more can you say?

"So am I. But life goes on. Enough about me. What about you? Where's that woman you were with in Jasper, in the spring? She your wife?"

Never underestimate the powers of observation of a waitress, you think.

"No, she's not my wife. Someone else's."

"Oh," Frannie says.

"She's gone. She went away."

You begin to unravel what you understand about what happened to you during those four months. You keep it short and to the point. You are finished your story in less than two minutes. But Frannie begins to ask questions. She does not ask it directly, but it seems she wants to know if you're available in your heart.

At 2 a.m., Nick brings over a nightcap, a bottle of wine. He sits down and has a glass with you and then he stands up.

"Will you lock up, Frannie? I've got to go into town tomorrow. It's been a long day."

By five in the morning you're exhausted. You hug at the door of Frannie's cabin and she kisses you on the mouth. It's a kiss that lingers a fraction of a second beyond friendly. You walk back to your cabin just slightly above the ground. You're dizzy with the possibility of this new connection. You're beyond tired but don't want this feeling to end. Frannie's perfume has a faint cinnamon edge. It's subtle but spicy.

When you finally feel you must sleep, you can't sleep. You are surrounded by her smell. It's on your clothing, on your skin. When the chambermaid knocks on your door at 9:00 a.m., you shout through the door that you don't need anything and head for the shower. In the streaming hot water you realize you want Frannie to be in your life. You also realize she's probably not available. She's swimming in a pool of grief and you have no fantasies of being a lifeguard. You only wish for her to save herself. Perhaps you've been drawn to someone exactly like you.

(40)

arriving late at the hot springs

Some time after
a three-in-the-morning walk
in mountain rain

after driving four hours
ghosts of elk, hazy rumps of deer
almost seeing the others
in ditch-bottoms lurking

after hunching over the wheel
desperate to see to the dotted yellow
heart of the road
through the slashing rain

after the very bad Edson coffee
listening to American all-night talk shows
from Seattle, Washington, Vancouver,
radio waves bounced under the bellies of thickening clouds

Driving by Obed Summit without seeing the sign
and I always notice that sign

after thinking there might be streaks of it
there, in that rock, along that tree, in that ditch

after arriving
walking through bottom-valley clouds
breathing the calm cool of this high retreat

after all this
at around five in the morning,
it finally begins to snow

eight Herr Schlemlacker

Balding, gray and ill-tempered, Herr Dieter Schlemlacker is the proprietor of a shop simply called *Fine Cigars*. Your first four times in the store, old Dieter virtually ignored you. He was such an ugly troll of a man. That's what you thought when you first saw him. Something was off about him and it wasn't just his pockmarked face and gruff mannerisms. He was the kind of person almost everybody did a double take on—they'd look and then quickly look again. He seemed to be operating in another space. His timing was irrational. When you looked at him he seemed to be a few micro-fractions of a second behind, or ahead.

You could not say Herr Schlemlacker was a fat man yet there was a certain girth to him that would not let you think of him as trim. He wore the kind of weight built by the abuse of alcohol and very rich, grease-laden food.

Nick had strongly suggested you visit this shop to buy his cigars. He admitted to never visiting the place but he'd heard it was very good.

You find the store without much trouble. All you have to do is park fairly close and follow your nose. The faint smell of cigar smoke reels you in. It isn't unpleasant to follow this trail. You rather enjoy the smell, which is mixed inside a calm, July evening. A red awning stretches out to the street. *Fine Cigars* is spelled out in small black letters on the bottom edge of it.

The front door is ajar. Inside, directly ahead, are three men hunched on stools at the bar, smoking. Two more men on a leather couch. One of these men, has a gray beard and is holding a demitasse of espresso. A Churchill sits on a small table in front of him. You sure as hell didn't know it was a Churchill cigar the first few times you visited. Then, you simply thought it was big. The other man has a cigar in his mouth and is reading the *Globe & Mail.* Narrow beams of halogen light cut through the smoke in the room despite the abundant air purification. A large walk-in humidor with sliding glass doors and filled with racks and racks of cigars is to the right. Then there is Herr Schlemlacker behind the counter listening to a low murmur coming from one of his customers. He has a cigarillo in his mouth and a mug of something in his hand. You can only see it isn't coffee.

"Do I just walk in and pick?"

He squints at you through small twisting strands of rising smoke. One of the men turns on his stool and frowns at you.

"I have a list," you say.

Herr Schlemlacker doesn't exactly frown. Nor does he smile. He moves around the end of the bar. He moves slowly, carefully. You're not sure why. At the time you only found it to be perhaps indicative of Nick's explanation of cigar smoking. The assertion that you can't rush a cigar. He holds out his hand and you thrust the list into it. He looks it over without emotion after bringing half-glasses to his face. You're watching him. You would not have guessed he was permanently inebriated. He was steady and looked to be focused. He hands you the list as if it's fragile and then barely nods towards the humidor..

You walk in and begin to search for the cigars on Nick's list. As soon as you pull the sliding door over, the fragrances hit you. My god! The aromas! The earth, and leather, and moss all rolled into a musky humidity.

Herr Schlemlacker merely grunts as you pay. He does not ask how much each cigar is, not does he ask about its size. He knows exactly which cigar he's looking at and what each one is worth. He does not say thank you. Only one word. A question. "Matches?" he says as he carefully wraps the six cigars in a baggie and seals it.

That's exactly how it goes for the next four visits. You come at different times of the week and various times of day. Only Herr Schlemlacker and one customer remain constant. The man with the gray beard is always there. Always with an espresso and an unlit cigar. You never actually see him smoke.

Going to visit Dieter slowly became a Hannah-like experience. You could imagine her sucking on a small cigar and drinking too much coffee. She would fit here. You recognized it almost immediately. She would find someone odd to sit with and then they would be odd together. And you would look at her and be fascinated.

On a particularly frosty November afternoon, you hear the Greek Chorus at the bar make fun of a customer who had tried to light a cigar without clipping it. A young man had come in and purchased a cigar and then a coffee. When Herr Schlemlacker checked in on him, to see how it was going—a rare occurrence even at the best of times—the young man confessed it was not going well. He'd been sucking and sucking and even managed to get the damned thing lit but it wouldn't stay lit.

Well, the boys at the bar think this is hilarious. They all have a good belly laugh over it. As if they were never new to anything. As if they fell out of the goddamned womb with lit cigars in their pugnacious little mouths.

Not Herr Schlemlacker though. He doesn't laugh even though he told the story in the first place. "We all have to learn somehow," he grumbles, "somehow, we learn how to do it."

You feel sorry for the ignorant dope. It just seems mean to laugh even if the guy isn't there.

One night, before you are to go up and see Frannie, you arrive just after the shop is supposed to be closed. You just had too much to do. Cigars for Nick got pushed down on your list a couple of times. Surprisingly, the door is open. Herr Schlemlacker is nowhere to be seen nor is the ever-present man with the gray beard.

"Hello?" you say.

Herr Schlemlacker appears from around the corner with a bottle of whiskey in his left hand. He looks at you as if you were expected. He isn't startled. He's not surprised to see you.

"I know you're supposed to be closed but I thought…"

He walks past you to the door and locks it. He pulls the blind.

"Now we are closed."

"But…"

"…You have, of course, another list?"

"Yes."

"Please help yourself. I'll pour you a drink. Give me your coat."

"Thank you." What the hell is this? you're thinking. It's been grunts and asking only if you need matches for weeks.

You get the cigars. You're becoming adept at finding the cigars Nick wants and occasionally you surprise him with something new you've read about. Nick scoffs at the cigar magazines, with their ratings and so on. But you find them entertaining at the least, and often educational. Nick's humidor is a Tupperware container with a wet sponge inside and a couple of holes punched through the lid.

You can't find any of the smaller Romeo y Julietas.

"Are there no small Julietas? I'm supposed to buy anything but the Churchills." You feel guilty for standing there with the door open so you speak quickly.

"Upstairs. Come."

You close the sliding door and follow the man upstairs. There, behind a closed door, is a humidor filled with hundreds of boxes of cigars and other smaller humidors. The entire room is a humidor. Cedar up and down and across. My God, you think. This is the real store. Downstairs is just a front.

"How many," Herr Schlemlacker grunts.

"Four."

He pulls out a box of Romeo y Julieta Petit Coronas, places them on a table in the middle of the room. Then he turns and moves to a humidor along the far wall. He brings back a box of Robusto Exhibicion No. 4s.

"I believe I would choose za Robustos but it's a free country," he says. "Bring three of those Upmann Monarchs, on the table there. Bring them down with you also."

You pick four evenly coloured Robustos and three of the Upmanns. You do not pick the four Robustos in the same colour spectrum for any other reason but aesthetics.

When you arrive downstairs, Herr Schlemlacker is reclined on the leather couch, his eyes shut. A coffee mug is on the end of the bar filled to the brim with scotch. Jesus, you think. Most guys who drink that volume of alcohol wouldn't have bothered with a glass. You place the cigars on the counter and pick up the mug. You have to focus on getting the mug to your lips without spilling.

"I've been watching you, ja? Watching the cigars you choose. The cigars you choose move through intricate patterns of taste." He does not move. Does not open his eyes.

"Most of them aren't for me."

"The lists!" Herr Schlemlacker shouts. "Yes, I have seen your lists!" He leans up out of the couch and points at the cigars on the counter. He tells you to wrap them up, all except two of the Upmanns. He burp-growls, a low guttural sound.

"But the Upmann is not on my list." He's pissed, you think. The guy has been pissed since the first time you saw him. That's why he seems so bloody off. It's as if he's been oddly dubbed into this life and this time by someone from another culture.

"The list! Always with za list! Bring za Upmanns!" he pulls a simple yet elegant silver cutter out of his pocket and clips both cigars. He carefully places your cigar on the table. You think about that. Handing a cigar to someone you barely know is an awkward thing. How does the person receiving the cigar hold their cigar?

How do you give it to them comfortably? Herr Schlemlacker's courtesy does not go unnoticed. But it takes a while for you to really see it.

He watches you as you light your cigar. It's 9:35 p.m. You know this because you were going to catch a ten o'clock movie with Sidney. You checked your watch when you came downstairs and thought you could just make it if you drove like an idiot. You smoke your cigars in silence. Herr Schlemlacker closes his eyes and smokes. His drink is cupped in his left hand.

Again, you can't help thinking about Hannah. This is one of the moments in which you drifted towards her. It was safe to be with her inside moments like this. It's the kind of experience she'd understand. Weird yet pleasing. Uncomfortable yet filled with a sort of tranquillity. An experience, which, if you were not in the moment, jarred you into the details of the moment. At 10:05 p.m., Herr Schlemlacker opens his eyes and says: "We drink out of such mugs because I have not a license to serve alcohol."

"It's the way I like it."

"Good. Yes, good." He smiles at you like you're a good son. Like you've just hit a home run or something.

Sitting in a pleasant smoky silence you eventually finish your cigar and the drink. When you go to stand up, you sway a little. You've got the booze and the nicotine from the cigar running through your body. You almost giggle but decide Herr Schlemlacker would not approve. It would be a healthy idea to grab a cab, pick the car up in the morning. You can hardly wait to tell Frannie. You'll see her tomorrow but want to call her when you get home.

Herr Schlemlacker tells you that you will pay the next time. He knows what you owe. He trusts you will not forget. The Upmanns were a gift. You look up the Upmann the next day. It's rated a 94 in *Cigar Aficionado*. Practically a classic.

You thank him for the cigar and the drink. It was a fine cigar, you tell him.

At the door, Herr Schlemlacker stops you, holds your arm for a second.

"Tell Nick the Upmann is from an old friend," he says. "Good night."

⊱⊰

Does Hannah take lovers? She probably continues to look for what is missing in her life. Your ego wants you to believe that after you, she is celibate. That after you, Hannah becomes a nun in spirit. Or, she takes lovers but they all remind her of you. Nobody ever said the ego was a beautiful thing. You hope she finds refuge with somebody. But at this point in time you'd rather not know. Perhaps someday, a letter will arrive and she will have moved beyond the memory of you. She will tell you stories about the new lovers. And she will lie. She'll say she thought of you. And you'll believe her. She'll weave her magic tales filled with imagery and metaphor, layered upon metaphor and rich imagery, and you'll be drawn in. And in no time, you'll be flailing around in a net gasping for air and wondering how in the hell you got there.

⊱⊰

It seems you are not able to become cynical or even bitter about anything having to do with Hannah. But you do not look at everything. You focus very carefully.

⊱⊰

At first, you thought Herr Schlemlacker was a send-up. With all his goddamned German inflections and backward pronunciations, you thought he was way too cliché to be real. But he is real. He's the real thing. He just is who he is.

⊱⊰

You never found out what was dark and ugly back there. You wouldn't even speculate. You brushed against it in the dark a few times. Hannah would not talk about it and you respected her privacy. It would have made it difficult to have anything tangible with her. To have real life with that thing lurking there like a land mine. Easy to lose a leg. If you could have, you would have gone down that path with Hannah and discovered what was back there. Perhaps together you could have put it to rest and not lost any limbs. You suspect it would not have been very romantic.

⊱⊰

"I've not spoken with him for a great many years," Nick says. "I only half suspected he was there. Marta used to keep in touch with his ex-wife."

You want to ask why but stop yourself. How was it that Dieter Schlemlacker could know it was Nick ordering cigars? How well do you have to know someone to tell who they are by reading lists of cigars? Did Nick ever write out a list for you? Was it from Nick's handwriting that Dieter figured it out? They must have been close at one point. You have a lot of questions. But Nick gets more silent than usual. He recedes into himself and then retreats from the table to do odd jobs. "I think cabin eight needs some new shingles," he mutters.

You sit there alone with your coffee. Frannie fills your cup on the way to take an order.

"You all right?"

"Herr Schlemlacker. Nick doesn't want to talk about him."

"Perhaps there's nothing to talk about."

"Perhaps."

You imagine it's a woman. Maybe a woman named Chiara Dezzia. There's a good exotic name. You found this name in a magazine in your dentist's reception area. You imagine that Nick and Herr Schlemlacker both loved her. What did she look like? Well, dark eyes. Blond, cropped hair. Full lips even when she pulled the corners of her mouth back to smile. She smiled without showing her teeth. Oh, there was nothing wrong with her teeth. It was just the way she smiled.

She was a climber. There's probably a goofy picture of her with white sun-screen goop all around her mouth so that her lips don't burn from the sun reflecting off ice and snow. They all met through a shared love of climbing in the early '60s. Perhaps they climbed some minor peaks in Italy and Austria.

Chiara was torn. She couldn't decide between the two men. They both loved her and she couldn't decide. The archetypal story of love and three people.

Forty years later Nick is living in the mountains, climbing and running around like a bigger than life Hemingway character, and Dieter is selling cigars on 109 Street, slowly drinking himself to death. Chiara is married, has five children and lives in Chicago. She's fat and has a mustache she just can't get rid of.

Frenzy. That's what you felt when you were with Hannah. You were barely able to function in the real world. Working and sleeping, and eating were only transitions to Hannah.

In your experience, frenzy is addictive.

Frenzy n., & v.t. **1.** n. mental derangement, temporary insanity, paroxysm of mania; delirious fury or agitation, wild folly.

The night you smoked the Upmann with Herr Schlemlacker, the ice was shattered. You became part of the established inner sanctum at *Fine Cigars.* And because of your connection to Nick, you sensed an affection born before it should have been. Realistically, you should not have felt so close to Herr Schlemlacker. You now have snippets of serious conversation with the man when he wasn't too drunk. And you always buy cigars from the upstairs humidor. You don't like being part of a group but really, the selection in the upstairs humidor is so superior to what is offered downstairs. You actually find yourself saying the word "splendid" when trying to describe what it was like picking out a cigar.

This morning, he is there behind the bar, pulling an espresso from the machine. In fact, he sees you come in and immediately draws one more espresso. He places it on the counter in front of you. Pushes the sugar container towards you with the back of his hand. A small motion of dismissal towards the sugar, an encouragement to you. When you don't put sugar in your coffee, he pushes it again. Again, you do not want sugar in your espresso this morning. And again, Herr Schlemlacker pushes the sugar towards you. Finally, you pick it up and place it further down the bar. He's talking to the man with the gray beard.

"You look tired, Dieter," the bearded man says. "Are you sleeping all right?"

"The frogs," he says. "Za frogs was particularly bad last night! Zay would not shut up!" Herr Schlemlacker automatically places a cigarillo in his mouth, squints as he lights it. Even though it's a cool morning and it's not particularly warm in the shop, Herr Schlemlacker is sweating profusely. He wipes his forehead with a tea towel.

What's he going to do with that tea towel? you think. Is he gonna dump it in a laundry bin somewhere? Or will it get hung up on the wall with the clean towels?

"Frogs?"

"Ya, loud frogs, everywhere! They would not be quiet. I got little sleep."

"Frogs outside your house?"

"No, no, no. They was inside the house. Everywhere. Loud. Too loud."

"You gotta cut down on the drinking, Dieter," the man says.

"Ja, ja, I know. It's not good." He steps inside the humidor and just before he slides the door shut behind he mutters: "but the frogs was bad. Very bad."

You look at the gray-bearded man and shrug your shoulders.

"What was that about?"

"Delirium tremens," he says.

"What?"

"DTs. It's withdrawal. He's probably been sober for a few days. He's hallucinating."

"You mean he actually sees frogs?"

"And hears them."

You decide this man is probably a doctor. You don't know many people who know what the DTs stands for. In fact, until that moment, you didn't know what it stood for. And there's something in the way he looks at people. He examines them like he's making notes. He could be a writer. Maybe he does crosswords religiously. Perhaps he's just a guy who knows what the DTs stands for.

Herr Schlemlacker steps briskly out of the humidor and pulls the door shut. His face is white. He leans against the glass. He's been sweating. Dark stains under his armpits. His hair looks wet. He's breathing heavily.

"Za frogs is in there too," he says. "Za fucking frogs is everywhere!"

nine

Noreen

Why are you involved with Noreen? Is it just that she's interested in you? Is that all it takes? Of course you sleep with her. How could you not after all the crazy stories about her sex life. You cannot resist the urge to taste. You're like a small child who's been told repeatedly to never touch your tongue to a frozen metal fence. Something drives that child to try it.

And it gets wild. It occurs to you that perhaps it wasn't Noreen's husband driving their sexual adventures. She attributed most of their play to him but in your experience with her, Noreen clearly led the way. And you noticed that leading seemed to suite her.

When you first look at her without her clothing you get a pretty good idea of the woman. A ring through each nipple, something pierced between her legs, and tattoos. The tattoos are everywhere. Some would say this is a plethora of tattooing. Is plethora what you really mean? Are Noreen's tattoos an overabundance? Not to you. Not something this beautiful. However, to most people, yes, it's an excess.

The patterns of her tattoos run in black flowing lines from her shoulders to her feet. There is no colour; only the black markings in various widths. These designs flower across Noreen's skin. Flowing irises caress each of her breasts. Her breasts are delicately held by these flowers. And the irises curve around on to her back. Graceful petals surround her belly button. Swirling vines draw your attention down to her pubic mound and then curve around, dipping low to grasp her buttocks in a swirl of hundreds of forget-me-nots. A soft rose garden down one leg and a myriad of daisies down the other. And always the vines.

The movements are spare, simple. Whoever made this garden knew about space. There are areas of skin where less gifted artists would have felt compelled to fill. After your initial shock, you find it amazing. This is not a motorcycle babe with tacky skulls or kitschy Harley Davidson logos. Her whole body is cohesive work of art. Someone has designed and created a garden on Noreen's skin. One beautiful, erotic garden.

Then there was the brand. You find out about the brand before you see anything. She'd been branded while absolutely stoned on tequila, she said. The scar tissue, on her right hip, was the burning imprint of an old-style key which was heated in the flame of a gas stove burner. It was before George. She was sleeping with a young woman who was into feminine dominance. Femdom she called it.

"Did you want to be branded?" you ask.

It's just before Christmas. You're together at a party in loft apartment in downtown Edmonton. You look out the window, down 104th Street towards Jasper Avenue. Snow everywhere. The streets white with melding and unmelding threads of dark tire tracks. It looks so clean. And here you are, standing with this woman who's been branded. Why would anybody want to do this to themselves?

"Well, yes. And no. I knew it would hurt but God it was a turn-on at the time." Perhaps she sees the confusion in your eyes.

"It was an incredible experience really. The feelings that exploded in me when the brand touched my skin!" She closes her eyes like a purring cat.

Oh my God, how do you please this woman? She's done absolutely everything and more, and then some. She has no first experiences left. What the hell have you done compared to this? She's like this invincible slut devil woman incarnate and you're akin to the Pope. You can't compete with this sort of history!

You look around the room. People drinking. A group of three women standing talking, their backs to you. One couple, two women, dancing. Noreen takes your hand and runs it up under her skirt, along her hip. The scar shocks you. "How did you not move? It must have been painful. You…"

"…I was tied up. I was tied up very tight. I couldn't have moved if I'd wanted to." Noreen stands back. "I like being tied up. I like the feeling of helplessness. I like having things done to me. I like rope. It works for me, you know, honey? She left me there for three hours after the brand. Every now and then she'd visit and do things to me." She stares off into the middle of the room. "I'm getting turned on just thinking about it," she says.

Noreen looks at you with those sincere dark eyes of hers. Her eyes always seem to be searching for something. Someone has started a Christmas carol sing-along in the other room. Why is it that pianos in people's homes are always out of tune? They're singing *Joy to the World.*

"I like it the other way too," she says. "I can be the mean bitch you've always been looking for. I can make you my girl." Noreen pushes you up against the window. You can feel the cold window pane through your suit coat. She's got her hand between your legs and she's squeezing while she pushes against you. "You have no idea what I could do to you. Or maybe you like the innocent schoolgirl routine. You know. The white stockings and little plaid skirt. White blouse. The innocent routine works for me too."

How do you react to these propositions? You're just not that wild. You used to think you were fairly experienced. How do you let her know you're interested in something with her while not sounding naïve or frightened, which you most definitely are.

Someone has cranked up the volume on a television down the hallway. You can hear Jimmy Stewart yelling: "Merry Christmas

Mister Potter" in the final scenes of Capra's *It's Wonderful Life*. You think just for a fleeting second that it would be an excellent idea to walk down that hall and find the movie. Find out who's watching it. Sit down and watch it with them. Leave this sex-fiend by herself.

"Well," you say. "You certainly are a capable talker."

"Is that a challenge?"

You smile. "It's an observation."

"Oh, I *am* going to enjoy this."

You're probably thinking that crazy sex with Noreen would be the antidote to Hannah. Being tied up, blindfolded, poked and prodded, and fucked by this wild woman would surely drum Hannah from your consciousness. Sure, you would continue to write the poems and send them to her but at the end of the day you would be cured. Noreen will be your kinky panacea.

What does any of this matter? Frannie, Noreen, your father. Throughout it all, Hannah is there just under your skin. Do you see the problem here? Hannah is becoming dangerous. You can't let her go. The memory of her, of that time, is not supplanted by these other extraordinary experiences.

You should be distracted by the death of your father, and you were for a good long time. You miss him every day of your life. That was a horrible day for you. Your worst day. There isn't a day that goes by that you don't think about him and wish for his company.

You should have been distracted by Noreen. You were, at first.

And now Frannie. Do you think of Hannah when you hold Frannie? Does something in the back of your mind wonder what Hannah's doing at that moment?

And death? Are you afraid of death? Your father is gone now. How does that make you feel? Do you feel that you're next? Oh sure, you talk yourself into thinking that death is merely a part of life. Life? Death? Same thing, you say. But you do fear that last breath. You understand that you will be alone at that moment. Writing and dying are solitary endeavours. You are no longer the teenaged idiot who thinks he'll live forever. There is death. Over there. Not far. What memories, what regrets will be playing in your mind? This makes you want to live. It makes you want to meet the eyes of the man or woman in the next cubicle at work. Or the waitress. Or that woman smoking with such bliss in the car next to you at a red light. Perhaps you are not a romantic after all. Perhaps you are an existentialist who clings desperately to a thin romantic thread.

(43)
the ride

I have entered the danger zone of caring
I have been lying to myself well, about this love
not admitting to anything but now
dwelling in this gray, wind-blown place,
where everything that falls to the ground,
is swept away; where clouds brood,
and the humidity is high but it just can't rain
And I was pulling it off, living right there
on the edge between nothingness/everything
where there is no hope, no future, but
just sporadically you
The careful curve of your face in dim light,
and the notes of your voice falling
to these adulterous sheets,
are memorized,
were memorized, by me

I have entered the danger zone of caring
I have been a trench-coated man on a hurtling train, who can see
the bridge is out over a vast and deep gorge
as a train pushes around a wide, pine-encased arc
and the train is engineered by a broken-hearted lunatic
who does not have an over-affection for life

I have been this man
who knows all these things
who turns his narrow back to the thought of jumping
who turns away from the lush green certain death ahead
who turns, and finds you,
and decides on the ride.

It means nothing. Never in your life have you experienced this. Love-making has always been an experiment in meaning, in making a loving connection. You've never felt the mechanics of sex, cold and callous, before. And Noreen did bring machines to bed sometimes. You've never seen so many dildos and vibrators, ropes and handcuffs, whips and blindfolds. You've tasted more odd and interesting things in the past two months than you will probably experience again in your lifetime. You even think that one night you weren't even making love to Noreen. You think perhaps it was one of her friends. It felt different. You're not sure. You were tied up and blindfolded.

You try to love but it does not show up in your love-making. Perhaps you were intimidated by Noreen. Perhaps you learned too much about George. If there's love embedded in this kinky sex you've not been able to feel it yet. You feel aroused, stimulated, excited. But love? Perhaps it doesn't matter.

In the end, you just retreat yourself from her. You stop calling, don't answer your phone, busy yourself with compiling a collection of short stories. Try to line up some business-writing work for the winter. Spend time alone. Eventually, Noreen gets the point. It's a gutless, cowardly way to break off but you just can't look at her and say good-bye. She might want to know why and you'd have to tell her. She's exotic and lovely but not particularly loving. And in person, you're willing to overlook the not particularly loving part. You'd actually tried to talk to Noreen about it to her face but instead wound up locked in a wicker basket with her.

It's only at three a.m., when you're lying in bed next to Noreen looking at the charcoal shadows of trees swaying across the ceiling that you feel awful and alone. Then, it's clear what you have to do. It's clear that you're not happy. But 3 a.m. is hard to recall at two in the afternoon, especially when a beautiful tattooed woman is walking naked around your flat.

You consider the fact that Noreen is available. Perhaps, like most men, something in you wants to be in love with a woman who is not.

You fall into a constant dripping depression, and a yearning, for Hannah. You doubt and wonder, and you continue to yearn for something you're not quite sure of. You're tempted to write her a letter but you've made a promise to yourself. Just the poems for a year. Hannah is something undone. But there's no going back to finish it off. Speculation about what might have been, or even what could be, is stupid. Just leave it alone for a year.

You enjoy the things you do with Noreen but they start to worry you. You worry about the possibility of not being able to go back. Once you do a thing, can you go back and find equal enjoyment in its predecessor? Having tasted Veuve Clicquot, can you go back to sparkling wine?

Here is a question you should be asking yourself: How does this differ from Hannah? All the ingredients are there. Is there something missing? Do you want to write poems for Noreen? Why not?

Do you remember the first time you made love with Hannah? Her hand on your back? The tenderness? Perhaps you and Hannah had something beyond sex and it happened very quickly.

Your understanding of love is complex and incomplete. Respect, trust, faith, friendship, growth, humility, compassion and tenderness. Notice, sex doesn't make an appearance here? Is that a problem?

You begin to ask yourself if this pushing of boundaries is the logical extension of love-making. Is this sexual pushing of limits the normal extension of any sexual relationship? Does everybody in the world go on this journey? Well, that's the dumbest question you've conjured up in a long time. The people on this planet who spend all day in a desperate search for food and shelter certainly aren't worried about the outer extensions of sex. Your explorations are a decadent luxury.

You can't even think about the things you've done in specifics. You lump them in vague terms. Noreen would not be pleased. She liked to talk in great detail while having sex. She provided a running commentary on the events which were transpiring. It was beyond sleazy porno flicks dialogue. Noreen was inventive and she knew how to create an erotic image. She was always coming up with scenarios and then trying to sell them to you. "What if I was doing this to you…" or "What if we were in the washroom of a Greyhound bus and I was…" or "Tomorrow, I'm coming to your office wearing a trench coat and nothing else. I hope you have a lock on your door…"

Lately she'd been talking about bringing another woman into the bed. She really wanted to hire a prostitute to come and do things to you while she watched. "Well, maybe I'll join in…who knows," she'd said. While that idea excites you to a certain degree, you're also thinking about what the hell you've gotten yourself into? Where's the end? What's waiting at the end of this journey?

Communication, you think. It comes down to communication. Perhaps Noreen keeps going off the deep end of sex because she believes it pleases you and therefore will be viewed by you as an act of love. Love dressed up to look like sex and sex misconstrued as love. You go right along with her because you think she needs to go there. You don't really talk about sex. You banter, and cajole and tease but you don't actually discuss.

You know how to juggle. You taught yourself. Thought it would be an interesting thing to be able to do. Three balls only. You've not pushed it to four. Four balls in the air is a step beyond your reach. It makes no sense to you. Just like juggling three balls made no sense to you before you actually did it.

Oh, your father wanted you to be enthusiastic about hockey. And then he wanted you to be a doctor or a lawyer, probably anything but a writer slash gardener. But you could not see the art in the game of hockey. You could not see the beauty. Nor could you find any joy. Is there a word that means: stuck on the outside of things—not part of any group? Loner doesn't quite do it. Perhaps a tergiversator. Perhaps you chose to turn your back on the game, on the camaraderie, the physicality of it. You know for certain you did not understand it. No one took the time to explain the game to you. Had some caring soul taken time to sit down with you and say: Well, you can't pass the puck over two lines because… or, off-side is simply taking your body over the blue line before the puck. Simple concepts, but not to you at nine years old. You just didn't get it. So there you were, dressed in a lot of expensive equipment, over your head as far as the talent level of boys you were playing with, and completely baffled by the game. It's no wonder you wanted to give it up.

Ahh, this is not a digression you should be taking now. There's a different narrative here. You, your father, and hockey. The ironic thing is that you love the game today. Even through the obscenity of players' salaries there is ballet, violence, and a gorgeous velocity inside the game. Now you see it, twenty years too late. But it's not too late. You appreciate the game. You bring love to it when you watch it.

tergivers|ate v.i turn one's back on something; be apostate, change one's party or principles; equivocate, make conflicting or evasive statements

Over time, your limited juggling skills evolved into three distinct versions of the same trick. In one version, the first one you learned, the balls basically followed each other around in a loop—passed quickly hand-to-hand at the bottom. The second version, you learned by watching television. Somebody on a TV show juggled two balls in one hand in a small circle while moving the third ball up and down with their other hand. It was more a sight gag than anything. Officially, it probably wasn't even really juggling. It was just a cunning variation.

ten

No last chance

You call Frannie. She's the first person you think of when a small publisher out east sends you a request for your entire manuscript. There's an interesting observation. You think of Frannie first. Not Hannah. But Hannah is not available. You cannot call her.

Marta picks up the phone. She asks you how you are and what you're doing, and when you'll be back up. Then she hands the phone to Nick. He fills you in on what's going on. A grizzly sauntered through the resort grounds on Monday. A German tourist trying to get a picture almost got herself killed, had to climb a tree, lost an expensive camera, threatened to sue Nick, the province, the national park, and the Canadian government. When are we going to start advertising in Germany about how bears in Canada are not lovable *Gund* plush toys? How many Germans have to get maimed or die? A man from Cincinnati had a stroke in the pool. Will you bring some cigars up next week and please do not tell Marta? Do you have a pen? I'll give you a list. Okay, Punch. Three Churchills. Three, no four of the Double Chateau Arturo Fuentes, and bring a couple of the smaller Romeo y Julietas, not the Churchill. The Julieta Churchill has gone to shit.

And Nick goes on. The sheep are gone up the valley. Something scared them off for a while. The bear? Perhaps. The road is still very good. But it's not busy. People don't know. We have to spread the word. Once it becomes widely known that we are open all year, there will be good business. Yes, of course, I'll call Frannie to the phone. Why didn't you say so?

She's ecstatic. She's very happy for you. But there's a distraction at the edge of her voice. Then she turns on a dime and tells you she's not so sure you should come up next week. She's having second thoughts about everything. Perhaps it's not a good idea to keep seeing each other, she says.

"What? I thought we were…"

"…well, you were wrong."

"Frannie, what's going on? What happened?"

"Nothing happened. I've just been thinking and I really don't feel I'm ready to do this again. It's…it's too soon."

"But we talked about this. It's been over four years."

"I can't talk right now. I have customers."

"I care about you, Frannie. More than I can say."

"I know you do."

"Call me later."

"I don't know."

"Just call me."

When you hang up, you don't really care about your good news any more. The hell with publishers and short stories. The hell with writing and agents. No wind in those sails. You're becalmed and depressed. What the hell kind of game is this? Your instincts want you to pull back. You're not the kind of person to strike back when you're hurt. You normally pull back to reflect and lick your wounds. You usually lumber into your cave and try to decide whether or not to trust again.

The third type of juggling is magic. You don't understand how you do it, or how you learned to do it. Perhaps you saw someone juggle and mimicked their hand movements. It's sort of the same action as pulling a rope hand-over-hand, only up and down.

So, you got three oranges, sat on the bed, and began to try. Just threw them up there with that hand movement and hoped for the best. Eventually, like the room full of monkeys flailing away on typewriters, you got it right. One monkey, after a hundred thousand million years of random pecking, produces a Dostoevsky novel. You, after a couple of frustrating evenings, juggle three oranges, very badly. Each morning while you were learning, you made fresh orange juice in the juicer.

When it's done correctly, juggled objects will cross over in the air somehow. There are moments when all three balls are in flight. If you sit and think about what you're doing, you can't do it. You just have to say: all right, I'm going to juggle now and begin to move your hands.

The length of time you can keep this going is small. You have no compunction to practice, to become better. You're just not interested. This is good enough. You're not about to run away with the circus.

What is it that you control while you are juggling? There are a myriad of forces at work. Gravity, centrifugal force, velocity, logic. For a very short period of time, you are in control of a small portion of your life. And you only get there by surrendering any idea of understanding what the hell you're doing.

juggle v. & n. **1.** v.i. perform conjuring tricks; perform feats of dexterity (with several objects tossed up and caught); ~ **with**, deceive (person), misrepresent (facts), rearrange adroitly. **2.** perform juggling feats with; cheat (person etc. *out of* thing)

juggler n. **1.** person who juggles; conjurer; trickster, impostor.

You meet Victoria and her goddamned amazing green eyes in a video store in Edmonton. She comes in for a hug and you can feel her sympathy. You're not quite sure why she's sympathetic. Has she heard about your father? Did she read about him in the paper? Or is this sympathy because she thinks you're pitiful.

Your trip to Lake Louise with Victoria, when you were insane with Hannah, begins to flood your memory. You even yearn for that itchy insanity. Your spine twitches and that involuntary jerk brings you back to the video store.

There's a guy wearing a red Yankee's baseball cap, much younger than her, standing in the background. She makes no move to introduce him. She has to be with him. He's lurking a little too long at the edge of your meeting. Now he's pretending to look at foreign films. He's holding up a copy of The Red Lantern. Ha! You're not fooled. This guy's likely never seen a foreign film in his life. You decide you don't want to meet him. He looks like one of those guys who squishes your hand, tries to impress his macho manliness on you when they shake hands. You hate that.

You feel badly when you think about Victoria. Here was a lovely woman with whom you failed to connect. You could not see her loveliness because you were too in-love with a ghost.

You let this slip away.

"Still have those hip bones like razor blades I see," you say.

"How can you see?" She backs up and looks to both sides.

"I'm just guessing. I don't know. It doesn't matter. How are you, Victoria?"

"I'm having a baby. And I got married just before Christmas."

"That's great. That's really great." Wow, she must have waited a whole six months, you think. "I'm happy for you," you say.

Then you stand there smiling at each other, uncomfortable beyond the outer limits of awkwardness. You just want to get the hell out of there. To hell with a movie.

Then she notices the lurking guy with the baseball cap and brings him over. "This is Roy," she says. And sure enough, Roy reaches out and hurts your hand.

"Congratulations," you say.

"What?"

"Your marriage, and the baby."

"Oh," he says. "Thanks."

Your hand is still throbbing as you leave the store. What a goddamned mouth-breather, you're thinking. A redneck moron, complete with baseball cap. A walking macho cliché.

Outside, you take a long breath. There really is no reason to be freaked out about this. Ridiculous. Before you open your car door, you look up. You would like it to be one of your customs to notice the world more—to look at the world at times when you normally wouldn't. You're happy you remember to pay attention tonight. The night is held inside a becalmed indigo. The air is still and warm. You roll down the window before you get in. You'll perhaps go to the Bistro and sit at one of the outside tables and have a cigar. You make this decision before you get in. That wasn't such a bad meeting, you decide. It's not like you went out of your way to hurt her. She seems happy.

You pull out into the parking lot, shift into drive and slowly move towards the street. As you slow down and flip on your signal light a small Toyota backs into your car. You feel the bump of metal-on-metal and then the revving of the Toyota's engine as whoever is driving realizes they're not going anywhere. The other car revs its engine to the point of almost lifting your vehicle off the ground. Finally they give up. When you get out of the car she starts to yell at you. She's a small oriental woman, nervous and scared. She doesn't speak English. Or at least she's chosen not to speak English. She continues to yell at you. She starts to get very aggressive and this begins to annoy you. You'd like to tell her that this could happen to anybody but she's in your face with her siren-like voice, repeating a phrase, an hysterical mantra.

"Does anybody speak Chinese? Did anybody see this?" you say to the small crowd gathered in front of the store.

"Actually, it's Mandarin," Roy says and steps forward. Victoria is probably still inside. You can't see her.

A couple with a baby wrapped in a plaid blanket says they saw what happened. The guy offers a business card. He's a lawyer, you notice. You're not sure whether this is a good thing or a horrible thing.

"She says you ran into her," Roy says. "She says you were going too fast. She's saying that this is your fault." You look quickly at her rear fender sticking into your passenger door. The woman does not stop her high-pitched screaming. She continues to repeat the same few lines.

"Will you translate something for me?"

"Of course."

"Will you translate it exactly?"

"I'll get as close as I can."

"Tell her to kiss my fucking ass."

Roy manages to get her to stop for a breath and then says a few words. She calms right down. Her voice becomes quiet and subdued. Roy says a few more words and then she produces her license and insurance papers. It's almost as if she's apologetic or fearful. She is gone from the parking lot very quickly. You offer your hand to Roy, this time fully prepared for the overly firm grasp.

"That must have been a hell of a translation," you say.

Roy smiles, "I told her you were a Buddhist monk."

(45)
mango in mountain light

There are mornings when I sit with coffee
and bird song barely serpentines through traffic
The light is gentle through elms along the street
and there is a cool underbelly to the morning
Memories begin to spark and flutter

There was a high-up in granite dawn, sitting on stones above a
Mozart string quartet stream—a ceiling of fingered
pine filtering everything harsh, and five days
of fine hiking behind us.
Only gentleness was possible that morning
Even our voices could not resist.
It was time.

We were healthy, happy, and alive
our faces brown, legs hard, and acclimatized to the high places
We were about to eat a mango with a sharp knife.
inside that cool morning

We sat at the edge of the stream and cut
the dripping orange flesh from the bone.

Mangos are a heavy luxury when backpacking
and this one had traversed four mountain passes
wrapped in a sweater, while we moved
ourselves through snow and granite and sun,
waiting, waiting for this last pure morning.

In the spring, you and Frannie go for small hikes although you don't call them hikes. You stick to the valleys, and trails with gentle elevation gains. Walks. You call them walks. There's too much snow up high anyway. Only the valley's are clear and even then, you run into pockets of deep snow.

At the back end of Pyramid Lake, a moose comes out of nowhere, down the trail, scares the hell out of both of you. You only have time to think: *big, brown, fast,* and then the moose is past you and into the woods. In the first few seconds it could have been anything. You stand dazed on the trail with the musty animal scent thick in the air. The moose stops about ten metres into the woods and looks over his shoulder to make sure you're not coming after him. Or perhaps he wants to look at you because he doesn't understand why you're not chasing him.

Down by the lake, on a patch of grass, you eat your lunch. Frannie surprises you with a bottle of wine. She pulls it out of her pack along with the sandwiches.

It's just after noon with only slight breeze across the lake. Just enough to keep the heat bearable.

"I used to try and imagine what series of events could make me not love the mountains. What could happen that I'd never want to come back. Ever. I could never come up with one."

Perhaps you shouldn't pursue this, you think. What the hell are you doing bringing this up. You're with a beautiful woman, you've had a great hike, and now you're brushing against a painful memory. Maybe you sense there's something there not finished. You go ahead and open your mouth.

"I think you may have found it, Frannie."

"Hmmm." She smiles sadly into her cup.

"If that had happened to me, I'm…I'm not sure I'd want to come back." Stop talking you idiot! What the hell are you doing? But it's true. You're not sure you could live here after that. Maybe you'd go to the prairies, or the coast. You don't know how she does it.

Frannie looks up at you. You find her eyes and immediately feel like a thoughtless idiot. She looks around and across the still lake. "It's about awe. Every morning I'm awed by this place. No matter what the weather. No matter what I remember, I'm always moved by this beauty."

You're silent for a while. She moves close to you and snuggles into your body like she's cold. And then in a whisper: "Sometimes it's hard." And then in half a whisper: "Some days it's so hard."

When she calls back it's okay. Her panic of doubt is gone.

"It's just that I came here to heal," she says. "I didn't want this to happen and now it has."

"You make me sound like a disease."

"You are, you bastard. You're in me and I don't know the cure."

"I think it's just one of those things you have to live with."

Frannie continues to push you away and pull you back in, push, pull, push, pull throughout the winter and into the spring. All through this accordion ride you stick with her. You hang on.

You've always been drawn to dramatic, melancholy music. Minor chords are good unconditional lovers.

They heard it before they felt it or saw it. A cracking sound, sharp and crisp. A cold repercussion. Three of them hang for a fraction of a split second in the air and then quickly follow the collapsing cornice off the edge of the mountain. Only later do Frannie's nightmares of what it was they might have been thinking during the fall start to haunt her. There was an eternity in that fall. There was probably time to think about what was happening. They knew. And the remaining three just stood there like stunned bunnies. Afraid to move. Afraid not to move. Eventually, in a sort of dull shock, they backed away from the edge.

No one was roped. Not on Cavell. Not on the East Ridge of Cavell.

The sun had pounded down all morning making the snow sluggish and grouchy. Perhaps the weight of the climbers was just too much. Perhaps it was just time for that section of accumulated winter to come down. The bite of missing cornice was big enough to be visible from the parking lot.

Bob and two others. Gone in seconds from that snowy ridge. And Frannie had maintained her anger up until that moment. She does not even remember what she was angry about. He was making gestures of peace. He was doing things to show his love all the way up that mountain and she was playing the role of angry woman. There would be no reconciliation. No last chance to say *I love you.* It was done.

You do not send the last poem. There is no number 52. Nothing gets finished for you. You don't end it. You don't have to make a decision about your heart. You can stay in that sanguine purgatory for the rest of your life. But are you really happy in there? Or is there something small and ugly standing next to you?

Hannah writes you. In the spring. Near your birthday.

What we had was about not living in time, she says. Love is really about an enduring vulnerability. Love is about becoming human.

But she does not say it like that. No. She metaphors you, requiems you, questions everything and then folds around and hooks you until you are so in love again you can't imagine it.

All this while, at the base of it, is the fact that she is where she has chosen to be. She is with her husband and their children but thoughts of you rage through her without permission. The second she steps away from that family world, you rise up. There is nothing to be done, she writes. Hopeless romantics all. Beautiful beyond belief because of its absurd impossibility. But nothing. Questions. Second thoughts. Yearning. Madness.

You wander around for days in a sort of shock. A lugging of words. A permanent lag.

There it is. There is the reason Hannah became a nuclear explosion in your life. Because it is impossible. Because she was impossible. Because the two of you together were impossible.

eleven

"...at the hour of our death"

You love the movie *Lost Horizon.* You loved it when you saw it as a child and you keep on loving it. The idea of stepping through that jagged portal into a place of peace and beauty intrigued you. It captured your imagination. Living in a winter climate only added to the appeal of that hidden nest. The idea of Shangri-La still draws you but you know if you want to experience it, you have to create it yourself. You've begun to toy with the idea that Shangri-La might be a temenos inside of you. You have to take a few steps towards the idea and hope the desired effect meets you in the middle somewhere.

Or you might be with the right person at a certain point in both your lives, and because it's the right time an obtuse fusion occurs. The light becomes altered. You might look around the room and notice a softening; all the hard edges disappear. Some might call this event being in love. But it's more than that.

One thing is certain: there will be no wandering through snowy mountain passes and the eventual stumbling upon a hidden sanctuary. There are real places you can go where you feel you're close to breathing the heady air of a quasi-Shangri-La. There are real places you've found where you can wake up in the morning and look out with wonder. You've been ensconced on a cliff in a climber's hut up in the Bugaboos, with a glacier tonguing out a valley below you. And you've parked your car in a tiny campsite which rests in the shadow of a massive icefield. In the day you'll sit and write, or draw, or read at a sturdy wooden table, your coffee beside you. If it's too cold, you'll sit in the cook house with a steady fire in the stove. The wind and the pines, and a few birds will keep you company. And every now and then you'll look up through resolute stunted pines and see the cold, angular line of mountains. Perhaps you'll feel lucky. There are days when you'll feel blessed. On these days you might feel hopeful about human beings, about life.

Who was it that told you about the word *temenos*?

Temenos is the Greek word for sacred space, a sheltered place open to the divine presence. A place that is protected from the habitual routines of the outside world. Perhaps a place for active reflection.

Close your eyes. Relax. Take a sip of whatever you're drinking. Go on. Do it. If you don't have a drink, put this book down on the sofa and get one. Juice will do. Scotch and water is better. This story will wait. Seriously. Get up and make yourself a drink. Put it close by so you can drink while you're remembering. Think about being at the icefields camp in a good spot far from the highway. It's cold but the cookhouse has a good fire going and you have just come back from walking to the toe of the glacier along the highway. Can you hear the steady hushing of Wilcox Creek? Imagine that grounding shhhhh sound as you lie in your tent ready for sleep. Does that sound of water over rock rise up in your memory? Do you remember being there in the fall as the meadows turned colours you could never hope to describe with any clarity? Lemon. Burnt pumpkin orange. Santa Claus red. Pure chestnut. Burgundy. Cigar brown. Beaujolais. Merlot. Ten-year-old Cabernet Sauvignon.

There will be only certain friends you can bring here. Only friends who understand silence. Friends with whom you can hike, or not. Friends who understand that simply being here is enough. In the city, in the middle of a summer heat wave, you will crave the possibility of snow at this place. While scraping snow from your car window, in the center of an icy cold winter, you will yearn for this raw green aliveness.

The Elk Pasture, with its cluster of cabins and '50s style motel, and two-minute walk to the hot springs, is quickly becoming a Shangri-la for you. You're thinking about that as you drive the twisting roller-coaster road to the tiny resort. You're going to see Frannie. You're anxiously pleased. She was angry with you yesterday because you did something horrible to her in a dream. Can you imagine being held responsible for something you did in someone else's dream? Regardless of the illogical basis for her emotions, she sounded angry on the phone. By mid-afternoon, she had calmed down enough to tell you that you'd gone off with some other woman, left her waiting somewhere.

You're wondering who it was in her dream that you went off with. Was it Hannah? Someone who looked like Hannah? Do Frannie's dreams have a recognition of your lovely ghosts?

You're thinking about utopias. You've been reading Krishnamurti. You've begun to think perhaps Krishnamurti might have approved of Shangri-La. Time and the right environment to learn yourself. But perhaps it was too isolated from the real world. Perhaps there wasn't a true freedom. Krishnamurti would not have approved of that. But wasn't the plan to spread into the rest of the world after mankind finished with all the killing and war and general perdition?

"What the hell is that?"

At the bottom of the steepest hair-pin turn, a car has hopped the embankment and is sitting in the middle of a small clearing enclosed by trees on three sides. You're surprised it didn't roll over or slide into the creek. At some point, the car must have been airborne.

The clearing is surrounded by an amphitheater of rising pine. The creek runs at its edge, follows the road and eventually drains into the Elk River.

Four women stand in front of the car looking at it. They're all wearing navy blue trench coats. A small gathering of secret service agents, you think. That kind of gets you smiling and then you stop yourself because someone might be hurt. You'd better wait until you know everyone is all right and you're far down the road before thinking about how funny it looks.

You pull over and park down and around the corner a bit. As you push the car door shut and turn towards the women, you can see one of them is quite old. You guess early eighties. The other two, when you get close enough to see better, are perhaps in their forties or fifties. The last woman is young. You only get a quick look at her. You never actually see her face. As you approach, she turns and walks purposely towards the far end of the clearing. She seems to be taking it all in as she walks. Not missing a thing. She pauses once, bends over to observe something on the ground. Then she stops at the farthest point from the car and just stands there looking upwards. Is she praying? What?

"Do you need help?"

One of the middle-aged women, wearing black hiking boots, says: "We missed the turn."

"Yes, I see. Are you all right?"

"We're all fine." You get the feeling that this woman is capable of handling anything but might have been shaken by this.

"This is a dangerous corner," you say. "People are always going off the road here."

"It is a sharp turn. Most unexpected."

"Have you tried to get it back on the road?"

She looks around the clearing, then at the faces of the other women, then at you. "No. We actually haven't tried to start the car yet."

You glance at the younger woman across the clearing. She's looking up at the pines and aspens, and the sky. Perhaps she loves the mountains as much as you.

"We were afraid it might blow up. I know that sounds foolish."

"Same thing happened to me when I got in an accident once. I got out of my car and ran for cover. It was only a fender bender but we get trained by watching television. Felt like a fool. Do you mind if I try and get you out of here?"

"We would be most grateful."

You wander through the tall grass at the perimeter of the road looking for a flat area. There is a narrow band of flat ground but it'll be tight. There is also quite a gully to get through before the safety of the road. First things first.

You sniff around the car, a square, four-door job of some kind, steel blue colour. You can't smell gas. You notice the Quebec license plates.

"Could I get one of you to watch for cars? I don't want to hit anything when I pull out." If I manage to pull out, you think.

The woman with the young eyes looks towards the other two and says: "Sister Sarah? Sister Perrault?" The two move toward the road.

Nuns, you think as you slide in behind the wheel and jerk the seat back. More evidence in the car. A Bible with a broken-spine on the front seat, a crucifix entangled in a string of beads hanging from the rear view mirror. The dark trench coats. A John Grisham book in the back seat. Well, the Grisham doesn't belong. But everything else adds up. Are they *all* nuns?

It takes only a few seconds for the brain synapses to connect. These are the same nuns who hit that moose in Ontario and lived to tell the tale. But none of these nuns resembles the nun you've fabricated—the one who makes appearances in your dreams. Well, perhaps the nun at the end of the clearing but you've yet to get a good look at her. You decide to not ask. You don't want to know for sure that this is the same car—that these are the same nuns. You want the possibility. There's a dent in the front of the car but it's surely too small for a run-in with a moose. No, put it out of your mind and just accept the possibility.

You turn the key and the engine begins to turn over and then stops. You used to have a Ford. You remember what it took some mornings to get it going. Without really thinking about it, you stomp the gas pedal to the floor and crank the key again. It starts immediately.

The car is stuck in a mucky rut so you rock it back and forth: D to R, D to R, D to R, letting it rock a bit more each time, and then you're out and the car is purring on the grass. That rocking motion which must be hell on transmissions, is a guy thing. You've never heard of a woman actually doing it. Although, you could imagine a nun in hiking boots doing it.

You back the car up and then line it up to the opening. Getting through is only the first part. The gully on the other side will be interesting. After you persuade the car through the hole, you turn the wheel hard so that two wheels are in the gully and the other two are on the gravel shoulder. The car is close to tipping over. You inch along the edge, slowly angling the vehicle on to the road. Once the car is safely parked, you sit there for a few seconds thinking about what a miracle it was that they actually made it over the gully and the embankment and lived. Did the term miracle seed itself in you before you knew they were nuns, or after?

The elderly nun, Sister Perrault, comes over and shakes your hand. She does not walk like an old person. There is an unexpected recklessness in her hips. And what a face! Lines of worry and joy. And she projects a steady calmness. She has been watching for traffic coming up the hill while Sister Sarah has been keeping an eye out for traffic coming down.

They all thank you except for the young nun who gets into the back seat, shuts the door after herself and picks up her book. She has her hair in a pony tail but half of it has come undone. A flop of chestnut hair hides her face. She's probably in some vow of silence thing and doesn't want to risk talking. Maybe she's just anti-social or stuck-up. Perhaps she doesn't like the look of you.

You tell them to go on ahead of you. You say that you'll be watching for them but that the road is mostly straight for the remainder of the way. Sister Sarah even says a *God bless you* as she gets into the driver's seat. The car starts off down the road towards the hot springs. You wave. Did the young anti-social nun start to turn her head or were you imagining it? No, there was a definite leaning forward and turning but the movement wasn't completed. Like somebody put a hand on her knee at the last moment.

Sister Sarah rides the brake all the way to the bottom of the hill. Then you start to ponder a bit. Four nuns travelling to the hot springs. What on earth do nuns dress like when they go swimming? Surely they don't wear bikinis. Classic one-piece swim suits? You're tempted to go up to the pool with Frannie and have a look.

After their car is gone, you walk to the end of the clearing and look up. You're curious. What was so bloody interesting? You want to see what she saw. Maybe feel what she felt. You don't see them at first. But soon, you realize you are not looking at a dark rock under a tree. In the pines, about ten metres up the slope, is a mature black bear, its eyes glazed in your direction. There's a cub up in the branches of an aspen above. This large—too large for any comfort—bear, seems to be looking right at you. You guess it's the mother. The two bears are just sitting there watching you. The creek is between you. It would take nothing for this mother bear to be on top of you. A few seconds. You begin to back up slowly. They don't move. You have a friend who lived with a woman who was mauled by a bear. It almost killed her. You remember your mouth literally fell open when she showed the scars on her back. You remember afterwards, finding those scars to be strangely erotic. This woman became exotic and desirable in your eyes. It was a small bear that attacked her, you remember. You get a flash of the memory of those scars. And then reality. This is a very big bear with a cub. Oh God, it's all romantic and lovely until you actually face a bear in the wild. Jesus! Don't panic!

You keep backing up toward your car, always, always keeping the bears in sight. How far is the car? What if the cub decides it wants to play with you? Is the door open? Where's the key? The adult bear moves, shakes its head as if it's waking up from a trance, and then turns up the slope as the baby bear scuffles down the tree and follows her. They seem to disappear in a lifting of green. You're very grateful they chose to go up. You stop moving. Come to a stunned standstill in the middle of the clearing. It's quiet. Still. A small trickle of water. A distant bird. Listen. The ocean. The wind in the pines sounds like the ocean.

(46)
Being

it is as if
our skins lose mass
become ephemeral
translucent, liquid
An alchemy of flesh occurs
and I am insane inside this reaction
You are able to pass through
my layers,
blur edges
Things become visible through me
I words crumble, disintegrate
but your hands whisper
you enter I softly
tenderly center
where I be

twelve
Shuey

You and Hannah stay at a bed and breakfast in Tofino, on the west coast of Vancouver Island. It's your birthday. Hannah has surprised you with a flight to Vancouver and then the beautiful curvaceous drive across the island. She's just had three wisdom teeth removed. Bad timing but doesn't stop you from loving. You make love with her, with the gauze in her mouth. That's not very romantic. It smells of an unequivocal desperation. But your loving has always been desperate.

You go out looking for gray whales, about twenty of you, in a small boat, inside a persistent drizzle. Gray sky, gray ocean and a fringe of rich green guide you out to sea. The swells are huge. Hannah keeps checking to make sure you're all right, that you're not seasick. She's mothering you and you let her do it.

There is a woman wearing a canary-yellow rain slicker at the back of the boat. She sits alone in one of the outside seats and cries most of the trip. Maybe it's the rain but she looks so sad you cannot help but believe she is crying. She's not overly dramatic about it or anything. She just sits and looks out at the ocean.

The captain, a too-cheerful wrinkled and weathered stereotype of a wrinkled and weathered seaman, tells you she's a fairly well-known singer-songwriter. "She writes songs about dogs," he says, "and hockey. She has a grand song about hockey. She's pretty famous all right."

At one point, someone thinks they see a whale. Everybody rushes outside—out from shelter—to look at the dark green rising and falling. The swells are massive inhalations and exhalations. Nothing but water, above, and below, and in between. After everyone goes back inside, you linger. The pretty famous singer looks up at you and smiles. "Hmm, what wasn't that?" she says.

You smile back. You'd like to ask her what's wrong. You don't care that she's pretty famous. Sadness is sadness no matter who's wearing it. But instead, you move back inside trying to figure out what just happened. She was commenting on the absence of whales. The way she said it wasn't mean or cutting. It was more an acceptance of what was, or wasn't. It makes you smile. You like her for that flat statement of truth.

You're grunting up Mount Shuey with Nick. You've chosen the gentle route which starts off up the valley towards Sulphur Ridge. Once on the side of the mountain, you stop at one of the false summits to have a beer. Shuey is mostly slogging up loose scree lower down, with sections of steep, solid rock as you get higher. Nothing technical. A good work-out climb early in the season. It gets the cardiovascular going. Wakes the legs up.

Nick wants you to tell the story of the nuns again. You've only told it a couple of times. In your telling, and re-telling of the story, certain elements become augmented. The bears remain the same but some of the nuns change. They grow in depth. The young anti-social nun grows flaming red hair. It was actually brown with reddish highlights. The older nun becomes rather lusty. A flirt. She only had the potential of being coquettish. The nun with the hiking boots becomes, in your mind, very fit regardless of the fact that you couldn't possibly know how fit she was. Sister Sarah remains the same. Well, perhaps she becomes a little more dour.

The four nuns were quite a crew. And they became more interesting with each telling. You do not mess with the bears. You tell the bears plain and simple. They were enough. No need to augment bears. And the young nun's behaviour at the far end of the meadow—you do not mess with what she did. Although, you're not exactly sure what she did.

Through it all, you low-ball your part. You did nothing really. You stopped and helped. The nuns probably could have gotten themselves out of that clearing without your help. You just sped up their departure.

"Ah, not now, Nick. I'm not in the mood."

"But this young nun, she stood there and stared at those bears the whole time. Stared them down!"

"Yes. The bears were there and she stood and looked at them. It was only after I got the car back on the road that she turned her back on them and walked back to the car."

Think about that day. She didn't run, or even walk fast. It was like she knew they'd stay put. Like she had a deal. Some sort of secret collusion with bears.

"What a woman!"

The thought of that nun staring down a couple of bears makes you smile. It has occurred to you that she was, in fact, protecting the sisters and you. That she stumbled upon the bears in hiding and made up her mind to keep them where they were. You don't want to believe she was petrified with fear—that fear kept her standing there like a stone tourist.

And what if she was not a nun? She was with a group of nuns. What do you call a group of nuns anyway? A gaggle? A flock? Oh Christ, stop being so damned sacrilegious. A group of nuns is a group of nuns. It only seems like there should be a name for them. Anyway, in your mind, she will always be a nun. Grisham or no bloody Grisham.

"Well, to the sisters then." You hold up your can and touch it to Nick's.

"To the sisters," he says.

Scrambling up Shuey's south face you come across three false summits. You have your beer at the second deceit. You've got more beer in the bottom of your pack.

You switchback across the face of the mountain until you run into soaring walls of indifferent stone. You go around the cliffs and up until you meet more walls. And then you go around and up again.

Near the summit and off to your left, a golden eagle hovers for a few seconds and then is swept away by the wind. Is that accurate? Did the wind do the sweeping or did the eagle make a decision?

You've not told Frannie about this climb. You gathered your supplies in secret. And you didn't tell anyone where you were going.

All the way up, you're impressed with Nick's agility. It's not that you were expecting a weak, feeble, old guy. You weren't really expecting anything but when he climbs, he's a sheep. He uses his legs thoroughly and sticks close to the mountain when the grade is steep. He appears to have more stamina than you. You chalk this up to the fact that he's completely acclimatized to this elevation and you're not.

You and Frannie are on the front verandah, bundled in sweaters. You're playing the Bach cello suites on a small stereo and drinking coffee. It's a warm spring day but the sun has yet to clear the upper slopes. Still cool down where you are. Water is dripping somewhere. In a few weeks, Frannie will have to move up to the motel unit for the summer. The hummingbirds will return from their long migrations to zoom and dive-bomb the tourists on the front deck of the lodge. The sheep will start to spend their nights high up on the slopes where it's safe in the summer.

You want to talk to Frannie about Bob and about how she's doing. You want to ask if the silt is settling, or is the water still murky. But you don't know how to bring it up without sounding like a heavy shrink. So you decide to talk about yourself. You'll talk about some of your feelings that perhaps mirror Frannie's. And then you'll steer the conversation away from yourself.

"Sometimes," you say, "I feel like I'm stuck. I stumble on Hannah, and can't seem to get beyond stumbling."

"But you're with me."

"I'm totally with you."

"But you want to be with her?"

"No, Frannie. There's just something that feels unfinished. Something frozen in time."

"Is she first in your heart?"

"She's first but it's only timing. She came along first."

"You know what I mean."

"My heart is actively engaged with you. Only you."

"Do you still love her?"

"Yes, like you still love Bob."

There. It wasn't exactly the most comfortable journey to get to a point but you'd arrived.

But Frannie's not done.

"Do you want to be with her?"

This is not working out the way you'd planned.

"No. I want to be with you." You stop. And if something goes wrong here, you'll have Hannah in reserve. Can that be it? But she's not in reserve. She's having a complete life—kids, husband, job, cats, dogs, hamsters, friends—all without you. What you have is a series of memories that you can visit and feel all romantically tragic and poetic and noble. You can go there and half-smile like you're some eighty-year-old man sitting in his wheelchair and remembering past love with drool running down his neck. You can get all wistful and sad with impunity. You can go through your life and never take anything, or anybody, seriously because you have Hannah. You'll always have Hannah. And…Jesus, that's idiotic. It's like showing a beautiful picture of a loaf of bread to a starving man. Even if the picture is an incredible work of art, in the end, the man will die. He'll starve to death.

So now you've got Hannah rationalized into being an unfulfilling picture that ultimately results in death. Lovely. You've come a long way, baby.

"I want to be with you, Frannie. I want to elope to Vegas and get married in the Elvis Chapel of Love if there is an Elvis Chapel of Love. Hell, even if there isn't."

She smiles. "Can we bring Pal? And Nick, and Marta?"

"Sure, but they'll have to fly economy."

You don't write poems about your father. You just don't. Perhaps you are afraid of the fascism of sentimentality. Well, there was one poem but it stayed high and dry. Perhaps it's just too painful to go there. To look there would mean looking at yourself in a bright, very uncomfortable light.

It's a wonderful feeling to get to the top of something, even if it's a small mountain. You have cheese and wine. Nick's brought a bottle of the Cote de Beaune he likes so much. You can't begin to taste half the complexities he says he tastes in the wine. You hunker down out of the wind, which is cool and has come up strong. There's lots of snow left up top but you manage to find a relatively dry spot to sit. The unwritten rule is, that even if it's a warm day, you cover up when you stop hiking. The heat loss once you stop, especially in a wind, is phenomenal.

"It was so long ago. But I remember certain things very clearly." Nick pauses, closes his eyes, drinks wine from a tin cup. "A small room. A high window and the colour of the sky in that window. It was gray but it seemed to have no colour. A thickness to it. And then a woman screaming in pain. She was shot trying to get across to the West. Do you know about the Wall?"

"Yes. I think I do."

"It was a frightening time."

You frown. "You worked for the Americans?"

"I'd written some articles after the war. Someone in the White House liked what I wrote. It was nothing really. Academic booga-booga."

"Wait a minute. Someone in the White House in the United States?"

Nick nods. "They used me a few times as an advisor. But never after the stand-off. I walked away. I walked away. Never looked back." There's a sadness in his face you've never seen before. If sadness was a stream, you think, this sadness would be cold and black, and deep. It would have risen from under a mountain to freeze your hand when you reach in to pull out a bottle of wine.

"But you're Canadian."

"Dual citizenship. And I was well paid…"

"…that's incredible. I would never have imagined…"

Nick reaches for the bottle. He tops up your cup and pours the remainder into his own cup.

"There was a lot of rattling of swords in those days. But even back then scientists knew that the idea of full-blown thermonuclear war was just ridiculous. It just could not happen. It would spell the end of everything. We all knew that yet the games continued."

"And Dieter Schlemlacker?"

Nick looks out across the valleys. You look out there too. Sulphur Ridge is below. Still a little scratch of snow tucked inside one of the top gullies. Beyond that is the valley of the Fiddle River. Beyond that you're uncertain. Beyond this uncertainty, you have no idea. And beyond the place where you have no idea, is a hazy diffusion of cloud and mountain. Thrusting granite in front of more thrusting granite, in front of an infinity of peaks and valleys. You'd like to think these mountains continue all the way to Mexico and then through Central America, into Peru and Chile and finally Tierra Del Fuego. There are distinct layers of seeing from the top of a mountain.

You look over at Nick. Imagine he's looking back into the past, reaching beyond where he can see. Even squinting does not bring the hazy details of the horizon into focus.

"Dieter was also an advisor," he says finally.

"Our Dieter?"

"Yes."

"Dieter with the cigar shop?"

"Yes."

"And that's how you know one another?"

Nick gives only the slightest nod.

So, Nick and Dieter out there in Germany trying to save the world. The two of them on the same team, fighting for freedom and democracy. Or perhaps they were on opposite sides. Perhaps that explains the forty-year rift. That would shoot your "other woman" theory all to hell wouldn't it? You decide not to push on any further. Not today. There's an edge to Nick's voice now. You don't want to ruin this day. Leave it alone.

But Nick takes the conversation and turns left before you can ruin everything.

"Only one thing matters," he says. "We can be very important in the minds of the world, and we can be very important in our own minds. But there is only one thing that matters. The people we love. Never lose track of your capacity for love."

"You mean your family?"

"Blood only goes so far. I mean the people you love. Friends and family, strangers, even adversaries."

(48)
Eagles

He says he has been hiking amidst golden eagles, in B.C.,
near Nelson.
They were hovering just above my head, he writes. As I went up this
mountain they stayed with me. I do not know why eagles have been
labeled with the verb "to soar" he adds. It seems to
me it takes a great deal of work for them to hold those wings
out there

He causes a memory in me. I am climbing on the side of Mount Shuey. An eagle, just for a moment, hovers beside. I do not think this eagle is soaring, or gliding, or sailing, or merely flying. It's suddenly there, throws its quick shadow across my face and then fast across the mountain side and is gone behind a ridge of granite

Then he asks a devastating question.
I wonder how eagles die? he writes. And he does not speculate. That task has fallen to me. It has been falling to me for two days now. It is a question which continues to claw me. It is something I do not want to consider—cannot stop considering.

Do they silently fold their wings on some deserted mountain top and simply stop breathing? Does a cold alpine wind ruffle feathers—blow away with its life-force? Does it remain there as snow falls in September? How do eagles die? How does all that magnificent being in the air stop? The whole question makes me twitchy. I mean, do they fall in a long spiral? Explode into the surface of an indifferent mountain lake? Feathers like smoke. I don't want to think about it. I'd like to believe eagles transform. When they die, they become spirit. Leave no remains. Perhaps become warm catabatic winds across the skins of glaciers.

"Who the hell is that?"

Nick is looking over the lip of your perch at a small dot, far down the mountain, working its way up towards the summit. The dot is making the same choices you made as you came up the mountain. Whoever that dot represents has yet to begin the long traverses around cliffs which will lead to the false summits but it looks as if they will follow exactly the same route as you did.

"I didn't tell anyone where we were going."

"Well, neither did I," Nick says.

You're both thinking Frannie has found out about this climb. But that's ridiculous. There's no way she could have found out. You were very careful.

"Well, it must be a tourist then."

As you watch the small dot, you see it pause three times to rest.

"A slow-moving, out-of-shape tourist," you add. You are not tempted to pull out the small binoculars from your pack. Why? You'll see this person soon enough.

Nick leans back. He finds a comfortable position and gently lowers his head back against the granite.

You think about what's left in your pack. It's your code of mountain behavior to offer up whatever you've got to strangers while you're in the mountains. You've never been disappointed. You've always given and received these offerings with grace and humility. It has always worked out. So, for just a split second, you think about what you have left. Just in case.

You look at the small moving dot again. It'll be an hour before whoever that is makes it up here, if they make it at all. You lean back into the mountain. Close your eyes and concentrate on the sun. Invite it to penetrate layers of your skin. Focus on it. Drift with that warmth on your face.

"Well, whoever that is, they're moving slow."

You've been drifting in the space between consciousness and unconsciousness, half-dreaming about birds. You were flying over water with other birds. And it was effortless. A blissful dream.

Nick is sitting upright with a cigar in his mouth, and his beret pulled on his head. He looks like a wild Zorba and you love him at that moment. There isn't any place else you'd rather be.

You roll over slightly to the edge and look over the precipice with bleary, half-opened eyes. Then you are suddenly awake. You pull out your binoculars and focus on the lone climber. It's Dieter. It's goddamned Herr Schlemlacker in his goddamned black overcoat. And he's wearing the gold-coloured scarf that one of his customers brought him back from Turkey. You recognize him instantly because you've been in the shop and seen him come and go in this outfit. What the hell is he doing up here, climbing around in an overcoat? Yeah, yeah, ya, you told Dieter where Nick was. You thought maybe someday, after forty years, they could bury whatever hatchet they had to bury and become friends again. But this was ridiculous. A reunion on a mountain top. How did he know you were up here?

Nick hands you a cigar and the clipper. It's a given that you will join him.

"Look, Nick, I know who this is," you say. "I hope you're not pissed off about this. And honest to God, I never meant for him to come up here."

Nick looks at you evenly. "I'm too old to be angry, or to hold grudges. It's all right. He called me last week."

Relief sweeps over you. "But what the hell is he doing up here?"

While you're talking, Dieter stops and sits down. He's perhaps a hundred metres down the mountain. You only half see him sit but something in you senses it's wrong. It's too hard, or too abrupt. Dieter suddenly becomes a dull sack of potatoes. You look over at Nick and see he knows it too.

Before Dieter-climbing-the-mountain was actually Dieter, when he was just a little dot, something far back in you wanted that dot to be Hannah. Just for a second, even though you are very happy with Frannie, there was something illogical in you that wished for Hannah to be up on top of Shuey with you and Nick. She'd have loved it. Perhaps it would have been enough of a hike that she felt she deserved to stop. It's the top after all. There was no place else to go, except down. Hannah was manic when she hiked. There was some hard-driven measuring stick inside of her that would not allow her to rest until some quota for the day had been reached. The top of a mountain, even a small mountain like this, would probably have been enough.

While you wished it to be Hannah, it was ridiculous to think it was. You believed the small dot was some adventurous tourist.

⁂

There was something final and brutally hard about that motion of sitting. As if it was the end of something. You pack up quietly and efficiently, and then begin to move down the mountain.

You don't say anything to Nick. You're certain there's something wrong with Dieter. You're thinking that it's your fault that he's dying or dead. It's all your fault. The big dumb bastard climbed up here to meet Nick because of you, and now there's something seriously wrong with him. Another voice considers a more positive view: that Dieter was simply tired and sat down for a good long rest. But then the first, slightly louder voice says that Dieter is down there in the early stages of rigor mortis.

⁂

When you find the medallion, pinned to the ceiling of your car, there is no doubt about who put it there. This has the old nun written all over it. She had time alone near your car while you were sniffing around their car for the smell of gas. It would have taken nothing for her to reach inside without being noticed.

"Do you know anything about St. Christopher?" You're sitting on the verandah having coffee and watching the frenetic comings and goings of hummingbirds with Nick. Marta has hung feeders from the eaves troughs and the hummingbirds come. They zoom in and around the feeders all summer. You hold the tiny silver medal in your left hand. Nick, rubs his face and clears his throat.

"You should talk to Marta. She knows about the saints. She's always talking about this saint and that saint."

⁂

Is it true that when you save someone's life you are responsible for them for the rest of your days?

⊱⊰

Dieter is alive when you get to him. You look for that first. Even a dozen metres away you're looking for a sign of life. Nick is behind you. As you drop down off a spine of granite into a small clearing, you hear Nick's voice. "He's all right," he says. "He's all right." And then Dieter moves his hand up to his mouth. You stop in your tracks. He's drinking. Dieter is sucking on a goddamned flask of something.

⊱⊰

"Whoever shall behold the image of St. Christopher shall not faint or fall on that day. That's what was written above an image of St. Christopher in my church when I was a child."

"I found this in my car. I think it was pinned there by a nun."

Marta already knows the story. Marta knows everything that goes on at the resort.

"He's the patron saint of bookbinders, gardeners and mariners. Perhaps more." She has been wiping the counter. She stops making the small circles on the counter top. "He mostly watches over travellers." She pauses. Looks up at you. "It's a beautiful gift. And from a nun! A double blessing!"

You find this blurb about Saint Christopher on the Internet, when you get home: St. Christopher was a big man who worked for a while helping travellers ford a raging river, much like a human ferry. One day a small child asks for his help across the river. Perched on Christopher's shoulders, the child seems to grow heavier and heavier as they cross the stream. Once on the other shore, Christopher asks him "Who are you, that you placed us in such danger. It seemed like I was carrying the whole world on my shoulders." The child says: "You not only carried the world, but him who made it. I am Jesus Christ the King."

⊱⊰

The small St. Christopher's medallion and the young nun who starred down the bears in the meadow cause a soft movement in you. Something shifts. You begin to see your connection with Hannah for what it was. You begin to understand your faith. You start to truly know that there is more to the world than what you see and touch.

thirteen
fear

Fear and love, says J. Krishnamurti, cannot exist together.

You decide not to put this in quotes. Not now. It's from a book you pick up in a Chapters book store. You think the title, *On Fear,* is interesting. So you buy yourself an over-priced, dick-ass coffee from the Starbuck's inside the book store and sit down to read. Three hours later you're shaking. You haven't eaten yet today and you're too full of Krishnamurti. You've been reading about fear. It's not our job to "deal" with our fears, he says, but rather, just to know what they are and to watch them.

What do you fear? Stopping. You probably fear stopping. If you stop you become normal. Normal. You also fear being normal. But you're starting to open to the idea that everything extraordinary is perhaps hidden inside the idea of normal. Your fear of stopping is why Hannah made such a great impression on you. Everything was in constant motion. The second you met her, she was beginning to leave. Your perfect woman.

Maybe you should go back and make the statement on fear and love become italicized. Make it look like this: *Fear and love cannot exist together.* It's not your thought. It belongs to someone else. But really, Krishnamurti probably wouldn't mind that he didn't get the credit. He would have hated that you stopped reading his book and wrote down this line. But that's who you are. You write things down.

There is a little girl with her mother sitting at a table across from you. The girl is banging her foot against the leg of the table. A repetitious evenly spaced banging. You don't even notice it but her mother tells her to stop because people are reading. The mother's voice is thin and perky, and just a little too cute. She's talking down to the kid. Her voice annoys you far more than the girl's banging foot. You look at the mother. A smile like a hyena. This woman wears a constant squinty-eyed happy face. You imagine this woman folds her underwear, irons her stockings and files cans of food alphabetically. The little girl looks up at you, then at her mother. "I don't care," she says.

Good for you kid, you think.

And then you ask yourself what you're afraid of. It's a small gesture. A bird dipping its head shallow under water and coming back up into the bright sun. And then droplets flying everywhere when it shakes its head. That tiny movement is enough. Is there something there between you and Hannah that you are afraid to look at? No. Nothing? No.

It's all there you're thinking. Everything is revealed. There's nothing left.

You leave Dieter with Nick and scree-ski to the bottom. You take the big moon leaps off the face of the mountain to land in the steep scree, look for a new leap and then jump again. When you run out of scree you jog to the resort where you out-of-breath explain to Marta that she should call the wardens and the hospital in Jasper because Dieter has had a heart attack. "Dieter is lying up there. Half-dead. He needs a rescue." You explain to the wardens where they are on the mountain. A helicopter is dispatched.

You find out later that Frannie used to date the guy who dispatched the helicopter.

Frannie is by your side now. She's pulling off her waitress gear and tying on hiking boots. You're still trying to catch your breath, drinking water and wondering what the hell to do next.

Frannie looks at you. You've never seen such a determined look on her face. "Let's go," she says. "I told Dieter where you were."

Marta pushes Nick's heart pills into your hands. You take the small container and shove it into your pocket. You grab a sleeping bag, two flashlights, chocolate and water. You've got four flares as well—enough to signal the helicopter. You and Frannie hit the trail at a trot with Pal leading the way. The dog barks in the distance. It's eight o'clock. You only have an hour of good light, and then another hour of feeble light.

"I never thought he'd try and climb up there for Christ's sake!"

"I have a feeling he's going to be all right," you say. You don't really think that. You're scared shitless. You think you're running up a mountain to find Nick and a corpse.

"Let's go."

"He's going to be all right."

"You can stop with the positive outlook crap and lets get going," Frannie says.

You push each other on the trail. You're quiet for a long time. You have to stop twice to rest.

"I'm sorry," she says, out of breath and bent over, hands on her knees. You just nod at her.

You do not look at the beauty of the soft twilight on the mountains. You recognize the fact that you should be looking. Then you remember the koan about the man being chased through the jungle by a tiger who wants to eat him. Eventually, the man has to jump off a cliff in order to get away. So, he's hanging by a vine. There's a tiger above him and a tiger below. Just as he was thinking it couldn't possibly get any worse, he notices two mice beginning to chew on the vine.

You half-smile at Frannie. "At that moment, the man notices a small strawberry plant growing out of the side of the cliff, in a little nook. So he reaches out and takes a strawberry, pops it into his mouth and thinks: This is the best goddamned strawberry I've ever tasted."

"The point being?"

"The point being that when life gangs up on us and tries to distract us from truly seeing, that's when we should be aware of it. We should open our eyes and really see."

She looks across the valley to the slope, which rises up to Sulphur Ridge. It's got a fine silt of orange sunlight slashing across its incline.

"Do you hear that?"

"What," she says.

"Pal. Pal's barking."

"Shit."

And you both push up the trail at a full trot.

Sometimes, you wonder if you offer enough to Frannie. Her husband climbed some pretty damned impressive mountains. He was also an expert white-water kayaker. There was an edge to everything he did it seems. You do not climb. You only scramble and hike. You do not kayak. You canoe, as gently and quietly as possible. Bob skied downhill and snowboarded. You cross-country ski, with bread, cheese and wine. Is Frannie just getting a milder version of her husband in you. Is she trading down for something safer?

"Well, you get the grand exit," Nick says. "You're going to be fine."

They hear it before they see it. And then it is hovering above them.

"I..." says Dieter.

"I'll see you in Jasper tomorrow. Fine doctors in Jasper." Dieter half smiles. Nick thinks about Dieter's arrival. A small dot inching up the side of the mountain. And now this opposite departure.

Dieter never did like to retrace his steps. In negotiations, he always became frustrated when they had to go over some detail repeatedly.

The helicopter lands above them where the meadow flattens out a bit. Two people with a gurney begin to descend towards them.

You and Frannie have to switchback up the mountain, a painfully slow process when you're in a hurry. You trot when you can and stop for short rests. It would have been more efficient to move up at a slower, steady pace but you're in a panic. After about forty minutes, Pal comes loping down the trail toward you with blood on his face and bloody gashes on his flank. He approaches you with his tail between his legs. He does not whimper. You will remember this small detail about this dog for the rest of your life.

"What the hell?" Frannie kneels in front of the dog. "Sit," she says and the Golden retriever does. If a dog can look spooked, confused and happy at the same time, Pal manages it.

"He's all right," she says. "These aren't deep." She's pouring water from her canteen on to his wounds.

"What was it?"

"I don't know. I only have a hunch. Whatever it was, it's up ahead. We should be loud." Frannie leashes Pal, straps a string of bear bells to his collar and he follows along timidly for the remainder of the journey. He growls at every turn, which makes you twitchy as hell.

This is her first time on a mountain of any substance since Cavell. You have this thought floating just under your skin. You wonder what the hell is going through her head. But there are no cracks. She's focused on getting to Nick and Dieter and that's it.

You wonder about the nun who stood in front of the bears. Was she afraid standing at the end of that meadow? Was there fear in her? Was she saying her *Hail Marys*? Her *Our Fathers*? Was there a faith at work? You'd like to think she was just winging it. Hoping things would work out all right.

You'd also like to believe that she was repeating a Buddhist meditation. Maybe she was reading a book on Zen Buddhist meditation at the time. Perhaps that book was hidden between the covers of a Grisham novel.

⸻

You hear the helicopter before you see it. Frannie hears it first. "Chopper," she says well before you hear or see anything.

You've given good directions. You hear it land, probably in the meadow just above where you left them. You're still a half hour down the mountain. All you can do is sit down and rest for the last push. In ten minutes, the helicopter is off down the valley towards Jasper. You watch it disappear as the throaty thump thump thump reverberates off the walls of the valley.

⸻

Hail Mary full of grace, the Lord is with thee. Blessed art thou amongst women and blessed is the fruit of thy womb. Holy Mary, Mother of God, pray for us sinners now and at the hour of our death.

⸻

First, Pal growls for about the twentieth time. Then, there is Nick on the trail, coming down at a good clip, a cigar in his mouth. Light is fading but you can see he doesn't exactly look sad. More, an even determination in his face. Pal runs up and sniffs him.

"He's gone," Nick says right away.

"He's what?"

"He's dead?" Frannie is winded, stunned, shocked.

"No, no, no. He's gone in the helicopter. He's fine. We had a good talk. It could have been a heart attack. You can't be sure of these things on the side of a mountain."

"They found you all right?"

"We lit a little fire, made smoke. We'd better get down or Marta will have more of a fit than she's already likely having."

⸻

Frannie was there. You're shocked. Nick hadn't said a thing. It's just not a thing you can imagine. My God, she was there! You feel as stupid as you've ever felt. All this time you imagined Frannie getting the news from a warden. But she was right there. Saw the whole thing.

"I was on the climb with him. I was there," she says again.

"You mean you felt like you were with him?"

"No, I was really there. I was angry about…I was very pissed off about a stupid, small thing and then he was…" She takes a gulping breath. "…gone."

Goddamnit, Frannie. You reach out to her and pull her in. You don't say anything. You just hang on to her.

"And now I'm angry at myself. I will always be angry at myself for my behaviour that day. I was such, I was such an idiot. I was a bitch and then the man I loved fell off a mountain and died." She begins to cry. "I wouldn't even talk to him."

Nick tells you that, at first, Dieter can't speak.

And his face is a painful grimace. He's hugging himself stiffly. Nick wraps his own coat around Dieter's shoulders and waits. When the pain seems to retreat a bit and the stress in Dieter's face eases, Nick gently touches his arm.

"What can I do, Dieter?"

"Nothing. A fist in my chest, squeezing," Dieter says, out of breath. "Son of a bitch."

"There's nothing I can do?"

"Less pain. Turn the pain down."

They sit in silence. Dieter can barely speak and Nick has no idea what to say to his old acquaintance. He wants to say something about how the world is still sitting on an ugly amount of weapons but that we're still here regardless of the dangerous time we lived through. But the man could be dying.

"Well, we're still here," Nick says finally, feeling rather silly for saying it.

Dieter smiles, closes his eyes. "Ya. We are still here."

After a half hour, Dieter seems to relax. His breathing becomes more even. Nick has been giving him sips of water.

At one point during their wait Nick looks around. They are still quite high up. The light is fading. The landscape softens. The mountains become cordial. If one must die, he thinks, this would not be such a bad place. But that's not going to happen. He's not going to die.

"If I'm going to die here, I at least deserve to have one last cigar, yes?" Dieter reaches into his inside pocket and pulls out two Monte Cristo Number 4s. Slowly, he passes one to Nick. "You have a clipper? Use mine."

Nick recognizes the silver cutter instantly. He makes no attempt to hide his recognition. The Cold War is long over. No need for games. This clipper was part of a deal they had brokered many years before. "Are you sure this a good idea?"

"No. Not a good idea but the right thing to do."

They clip their cigars, and then Dieter pulls out a butane lighter. He begins to heat the end of his cigar with the steady blue flame.

"It seems," Dieter says, "that I am always doing the right thing against good ideas."

Nick watches him. Waits for him to catch his breath.

"In Germany…do you remember Charlie Checkpoint? A long time ago. I did not have the authority to make the deal I made."

"What?"

"It was the ending of my career. There were those who wanted to march into West Berlin and to hell with any consequences."

Nick thinks about what those consequences might have been. All out war with thermonuclear weapons we barely understood? Nothing? Conventional war?

"But you made a deal to pull back. You made the deal. *We* made the deal."

"Yes, we made that deal. It was the right thing."

"But not a very good idea for you."

"I was looking out after your career." Dieter smiles. "It was a small thing to pull back our tanks first." Dieter's smile fades away. "I..." But why, he thinks. It serves no useful purpose to reveal this now, after all this time. Why should he burden Nicholas with this weight? They are old men now. No reason to poison memories of that day with this information.

They both think about the woman who was shot just a few hours after the pullback. Dieter's sister had been sent out towards the wall and West Berlin as a punishment. *You may go*, they said. *You're free to go to the West. Your brother and your family will follow. It's alright.* She was Dieter's punishment. Her death was a devastating reprimand to Dieter and others like him who would consider disobeying Mother Russia. Dieter can feel himself wanting to cry. It's as if there is a pocket of incredible grief hidden inside of him, and he has just stumbled upon it for the first time. And really, he asks himself, who the hell cares if I weep? I am here with Nicholas. Dieter lets go. He yields to the grief and the tears for the first time.

Nick only remembers that anonymous woman pleading through the early morning hours. And he remembers his horrible disgust. Even now, the memory of that scene turns his stomach. He wants to speak his horror to Dieter. He wants to tell him about his disgust for the "isms" of the world. All the "isms." Communism killed that poor woman and Capitalism stood by and let that woman be shot. Nick is about to speak but he looks up and sees Dieter is sobbing. He is looking down at the cigar in his hand and weeping.

Enough, Nick thinks. Enough. He moves over and sits beside Dieter, puts his arm around his shoulders and gently squeezes. They become old silent rocks on the side of the mountain and twilight wraps itself around them like a weathered navy blue blanket.

fourteen
peripheries

Perhaps you let the observation of peripheries go too far. You can lose control of the peripheral elements. If they take over you'll lose control of the narrative. They can only threaten to take over. Walk up to the brink, make those peripheral characters think they're it—that they're the whole show—and then yank them back.

But it is so appropriate for you to almost lose control of your own story. Hannah was like that. She could be focused and driven but you truly loved her when she digressed because she digressed with temerity. So, who cares what happened to Nick and Dieter. And really, Noreen is such a small, freaky part of this narrative. Okay, you care about Nick and Dieter, and Noreen. But they're not the story. They stand at the edge. And the nun? What about the nun? You don't really know anything about her. Even the incident in the tiny meadow has a surreal quality to it. You begin to mistrust your own perceptions.

Imagine being close to the end of your poetry campaign. Shut your eyes. Put your feet up on a pillow. Pretend it's almost been a year.

Say, you've written 49 poems. Not all your poems to Hannah have been love poems. Some have been about the mountains or the stars, or that crow up on Tunnel Mountain who hung suspended inside the wind. Some of your poems were very short. Some were more short story than anything. Some were not about Hannah at all. A few poems came from memories that predated Hannah. But she was always your audience.

Now, imagine you have three poems left to write. What will you do now that you're done? Is there anybody new in your life?

Three more poems and then what? A trinity of poems to send and then you are done. Are you clear in your mind about what you want to do? Are you going to follow her out there with the possibility of ruining her life, and yours? Do you have the drive in you, the need to find out what can be between you and Hannah? Perhaps you are convinced that what you had was extraordinary. Have you explored the idea of extraordinary? Is it possible that extraordinary experiences are only delicate and understated? Perhaps extraordinary experiences fold over, and then fold over again like a snowstorm moving up and down a mountain valley.

In the Rockies, at certain times of the year it becomes difficult to determine if you're near life, or near death. The colours are deceiving. Withered brown grasses, the wine-coloured willow branches and the pale, wispy clumps of aspens. It was either October, before the snow fell, or it was April, after the last swatches of snow had melted. You know when it was. It was October. But the colours made it only a small step to imagine it might be spring.

Parker Pass is near the Skoki Valley, behind Lake Louise in Banff National Park. You were there during a hike, on your way to Baker Lake. Parker Pass wasn't on your map. You found it by accident and only later discovered its name. It felt wrong that day. It was mid-October but there was no snow. The entire landscape, the trees, the grass, the fallen granite, the mountains which rose straight up from beside the pathway, waited. It seemed everything was waiting for snow. At some point earlier in the fall, there had been an inhalation, slow and steady. And now, the exhalation was long over due.

You've climbed up the steps of granite above the pass, so you can see both vistas. You imagine a lover standing there below you. You imagine she is out of place in these mountains. She is city, through her bones. But you've managed to get her up here, to let her see what you see, feel what you feel, and smell the nothingness of pine-brushed air. Perhaps she doesn't get it. She just looks around and sees dull rock and too many trees and too much work to get there. But you imagine being in love with this woman regardless of her gray heart.

(50)
late fall, before the snows on Parker Pass

Turn left and up,
up steep steps of granite
through alcoves of stranded snow
to find the hard silence

I look down
from my perch
and you are tucked
into a small emerald ball
hugging yourself warm

You have made yourself a stone
out of place on this high
mountain pass
in your city leather

You become even smaller
amidst these giant sharp edges
these cold gray knives
that cut clouds until they
bleed stingy skiffs of snow

I want to place the pebble you've become
into my mouth, delicately roll you around
taste the wind, the late snow,
the mud on your boots
the withered grasses
your skin
your sweat
your salt

and I will take you with me
silent and still
when we part

So you take that poem and send it, just like the 49 that came before. You direct those feelings towards Hannah. Those feelings are not meant for her. They're not really meant for anybody. Yet you direct them at Hannah, she gets them, and when she reads them there is a doubt in her about whether they belong to her or not. She's really an incredibly bright woman. She can easily dismiss them at first. But there is a nagging reluctance to let go entirely. Perhaps it's just a single line. An image. A word. Is it: the pebble you've become? Is that the line that captures her fancy? Does she turn at look out the window in the middle of breakfast and think of that line? Does wistfulness imagine itself across her face as she no longer hears the radio, her children talking, the dishwasher, or a truck moving by in front of the house. She is a far better metaphorical visionary than you. She can metaphor circles around you. You've had to let go of that idea in order to send these poems to her. But today, today she is captured by that one line. The metal-grated doorway clanks shut and she jumps around to find herself trapped. She let her guard down. You do not belong here with children and laundry and breakfast. You are an away indulgence. This is the temporal world. And you do not belong. But Hannah let you in and now she must work to get you out.

There's always a delicate hesitation when you approach the Elk Pasture. You'd like to have been able to skip over the awkwardness you feel but it seemed unavoidable. It wasn't an ugly feeling. And it contained no dread. Yet each time you met again there were questions under the skin—questions that were never spoken.

"Hi," she says as you slip through the doorway into the cabin.

It's late. You're exhausted from the drive and a hard week at work. There's a steady fire going. It's about 3 a.m. Your hand automatically drops to rub the top of Pal's head.

Some of your kisses are perfunctory. But there is an edgy lust. And there is an edge of gentleness. There are many edges.

"Come," she says. And she takes your hand and draws you out into the cold night. Together, you walk the path towards the hot springs. There is corn snow over top of a thin layer of packed snow on the ground. You crunch your way through the woods and then come out in full view of the pool building. The only light is from the road where there are street lamps projecting cones of yellow at the ground through the mist. The pool is dark.

The front door is open. Once inside, Frannie locks it.

Where you are supposed to spilt off and follow the way of your gender, she pulls you in her direction. Together, you enter the realm of women.

Then, cold stars on bare skin. Moving through frost and fog. The small slapping sounds of feet on cold cement. Knowing that there is an immediate, blissful sanctuary from this discomfort, you purposely slow down, prolong, anticipate. Someone has lit candles at the pool edge. There's music. Miles Davis. A ballad weaves through the fog. Frannie moves ahead of you. She slips her naked cello into the thick water with hardly a splash. And then you are floating in a massive womb, contemplating your birth into a universe of stars.

You are quiet for a long time. And then you will only whisper. Only whispering seems appropriate.

This is such a wonderful gift after the drive.

"You know how there are moments in the continuum of loving someone where the love intensifies? It gets so focused it almost hurts?"

"Mm, hmm." Frannie is standing beside you. The water is just under your chins.

"I'm inside one of those moments right now."

From a bag, tucked under one of the benches beside the pool, Frannie pulls out a bottle of whiskey and two glasses.

"A toast then," she says. "To now."

"To now," you say. "No past and no future. Now."

Add to this scene the taste of the Laphroaig. The smoky flavour. The earth. Its caramel sweetness.

"Here we are. Waiting to be born," she whispers.

And when the fog curls over your heads it is a white cave. You can feel yourself getting sad. You feel sadness coming, a galloping horse, three galloping horses. A membrane grows around you, pulsing with blood. The colour red. Red does not belong here. You don't want to feel sad so you begin to push it back. You finish your drink and pour another. Then you kiss Frannie with a blistering heat that is entirely inappropriate. You have another drink. The harder you push against the sadness the more powerful it becomes. Soon, it is so huge that you can't even begin to see it.

It will take you years to understand that if you surrender to your sadness, accept it and listen to it, it will only linger awhile and then move on with 5 a.m. birdsong.

Frannie does not ask you what's wrong. She retreats into her own thoughts.

After what seems a lifetime, you break the gloom by moving into her gently. And you hold her and thank her for this sanctuary. And you tell her you love her. In the women's shower room, inside clouds of steam, you and Frannie make love. You reverse the drifting apart. Open yourself to this woman. Become vulnerable.

Were you re-born when you pulled yourselves out of that pool? Perhaps it was more a birth of traits as opposed to person. But then are not people made up of their traits?

Perhaps a determination to go on with each other was born. Perhaps it was a small inkling that this woman was worth any struggle. Nothing is born full-grown. Newborns require nurturing.

fifteen the Bridge

At the parking lot, in front of Mount Cavell, you see Angel Glacier suspended against the mountain. You can see why it got that name. Here is an angel with granite feet, its torso pinned to the face of this mountain, its wings back, body exposed to the elements. A cruel image. It makes you sad to look at this angel. You would like to get some plastic explosives, climb up there behind the angel and blast it free. You'd like to blow up quite a few things actually. You'd probably take out several ski hills, a few hotels which are particularly hideous, and most of the golf courses inside the national park. Given a lot of explosives and the wherewithal to use them, you'd also blow the shit out of most of the highways in the park. But you do not have access to plastic explosives. So you add it to your imaginary list and the angel remains. Eventually, you have to look away.

The Welsh have a phrase which means: lost and wandering soul. You remember hearing someone at the Folk Festival saying it. It sounded like: dune yer care. Lost and wandering soul. That could very well be you. Perhaps you are not meant to settle, ever. You begin to think about leaving. You imagine heading out on the road.

Driving for as long as you can afford it, then selling the car and moving on however you can. You wish the Buddhists were still ensconced in Tibet. Goddamn the Chinese for that. But there are still sanctuaries in the world. There is Thich Nhat Hanh's Buddhist community in southern France. A place to go and practice being mindful. You could just go to the mountains and do anything to survive. But you are already in the mountains.

You could change your status from frequent visitor to resident.

⋄

You're not exactly sure why you came to the base of Cavell today. Perhaps you both came to watch your fears. There is fear in this place for both of you. Fear and history. A good place to sit quietly and observe. There is a small bridge across the stream which flows out of Lake Cavell. That's your destination this afternoon.

You didn't come with a purpose of saying good-bye. You didn't come here to perform a ceremony of releasing the past. All this comes about spontaneously. Probably years later you'll think back on this and realize you let go of things in spasmodic jerks. It is never a smooth process for you.

At the bottom of a narrowing pathway you reach the sturdy, wooden bridge.

⋄

It's a thirteen kilometre up-hill drive to get to the parking lot at the base of Cavell. The Park Services people, in order to stop as many people as they can from visiting the mountain, have erected an elaborate sign at the bottom of the road explaining when you can drive your car up and when you can drive it down. They probably didn't plan it to confound, but it appears so. You're not sure, but you think they've turned the road into one-ways, depending on what time it is. The sign is, in fact, so confusing that as you were trying to figure it out you saw three cars turn around and go away. You remember reading about the degradation of the meadows across from Cavell. There are too many people up there who do not stay on the trail and the meadows are destroyed to the point where the Park authorities are considering fencing them in for a hundred years or so. No need for that, you think. This sign is a brilliant stroke. Completely closing the road to vehicles would solve the problem but it would take guts and fortitude to do that. It would be politically risky. Those folks in their motor homes hauling all their worldly possessions around with them might complain. It might be seen as discriminating against the old, the sick, the very young, the lazy, the slothful, the unborn, small pets, homosexuals, gardeners, telemarketers.

You look at Frannie and admit to having no clue as to when you're allowed to drive this road.

"It looks like it's open to me," she says.

You push the car into Drive and gun it past the gate and the idiotic sign. Sure enough, about half way up you run into a convoy of motor homes coming down the road—taking the entire road—who all honk their horns at you because they have to slow down and move over. You and Frannie give a special, one finger wave to each and every one of them and then giggle like recalcitrant children.

You look at the blank sheet of paper in your hands. If you don't do this, if you don't do something, you'll be caught inside that unwritten poem. You won't move on. You won't be able to grow. Operating on desire never brings about the right actions. You need to stop acting on desire. You've become quite good at it. But you hesitate. You don't want to destroy that place. You've convinced yourself that it's beautiful in there. The light is odd, as if it's been filtered through water, with golden leaves floating on its surface. You considered writing the last poem and sending it. Then it would be over. But somehow you could never quite start to write it. To be with Hannah inside a poem that was never written is a bliss you're unwilling to surrender. And that's what it comes down to isn't it? This whole adventure is about letting go. It's about attachments. But you do not need to let go of love. You do not need to let go of Hannah. Not really. No. There's something else. But you don't want to think about it.

⊱⊰

It's all there you're thinking. Everything is revealed. There's nothing left. But if you stop moving — and even now you are in constant motion with your driving back and forth from the city to the mountains — you fear you will begin to look directly at this story. And what will you see that makes you afraid?

⊱⊰

But that poem is already written. It is written in your life. And right now it is written with invisible ink. Or it was written on the page above this blank sheet, and there are only faint impressions. Or perhaps it was written three or four pages above the imprinted page, and you need a psychic to decipher what is there. Even the lightest touch of a pencil scratched across the page will only bring faint sketches of words.

⊱⊰

What's the real reason you didn't write that last poem? You're standing here on this bridge with a blank sheet of paper in your hands and the mountains all around and you still will not look beyond the surface. You will not look under the paper, through the fiber, the pulp, and white innocence. You have been telling yourself, over and over again that it's the journey of love you don't want to end. That may in fact be true. But it's only partially true. You know the rest but you will not admit it even to yourself.

It's about love, and yearning, and letting go, you'll tell yourself. It's about un-attachment.

But if it's about more than love, you can drop a hundred sheets of paper, a thousand sheets, a million, million sheets of paper into that black stream and you will not be healed. You must understand in your heart the reason you will not write the last poem.

⊱⊰

When you are climbing, or scrambling, and you come up against a near-vertical wall, what do you do? You are never interested in straight up. You prefer to go around. Around and then up. There's fear for you on the rock face. Your knees begin to shake.

Is that it? Is that the ending? You come to the realization that you only exist with Hannah inside the 52nd poem. You are with her and love her freely and with an insanity inside that unwritten poem. You are with Hannah totally and completely, ensconced inside a concept that does not exist. This is what you think about while standing on the bridge at twilight with Frannie. You reach out and take her hand. Her hand is real. It is not across a country. It's not inside a metaphor, inside an unwritten phrase, inside an unwritten poem.

You are thinking about all of these things as you hold that sheet of paper in your hand. A feeling of bottomless missing overwhelms you. It's the same feeling you get when you think of your father and Christmas at the same time. That feeling overlays Hannah. You are standing in a massive dark room with only the echo of your own voice to measure distance. He always complained about having to get up Christmas morning. It's supposed to be a holiday, he'd say. Jesus wouldn't want me to get up this early on his birthday. He wouldn't want anybody to get up this early. You kids just stay in bed until noon or one o'clock.

And the way he complained about all the damned presents and how these kids were spoiled to death. And that money didn't grow on goddamned trees you know! He complained about everything, left all the present buying to your mother. Pretended to be the consummate Grinch. But on Christmas mornings, there were always extravagant presents for everyone. Presents your mother knew nothing about. And these were thoughtful gifts. Gifts only arrived at by listening. And he was always up first, making the bacon smell float through the house. He loved Christmas. He loved everything about it. It took you a good long time to figure that out.

Perhaps your eyes tear up. Perhaps you cannot harden this. You think about your father and about Hannah. The missing in you becomes too much. You lean over the railing of the bridge and look at the fast, uncaring water. Frannie moves up close. She slips her arm around your waist.

"I know," she whispers. "I know."

⊳⊢⊲⊳⊸○⊸⊲⊳⊣⊲

But she doesn't know anything! Open your eyes! Look where you are. There is a loss here, more intense than lost love. You look at your father and at love in order to avoid something else.

Something was started and ended.

Something began. And then ended.

It wasn't love.

⊳⊢⊲⊳⊸○⊸⊲⊳⊣⊲

It's not like you hadn't thought about it. You thought about it quite a bit. In your love-bitten, stunned state of mind, you thought it wouldn't be such a bad thing.

But then she came to you, a knock at the door at 3 a.m.

It could be no one else. But why wasn't she using her key? You gave her a key. Why is she knocking?

"I forgot," she says. "I just forgot."

You draw Hannah inside. She allows herself to be drawn in like a sigh. And you hold her in the dark hallway.

She has a bottle of wine in her bag. She never carried a purse. Knapsacks, or pouches, or leather bags provided what she needed.

You look at her in the half-light and immediately know that something is being ripped in two inside of her. Something's wrong. It's as if her skin has been stretched to the point of translucence. She has no colour in her face—flesh tones siphoned away. You find her to be absolutely striking regardless of this physical ebb. And you know what it is. You know. You know. You know.

She draws you to bed, leaving a Hansel and Gretel trail of clothing down the hallway and through the kitchen.

⊳⊢⊲⊳⊸○⊸⊲⊳⊣⊲

"Don't."

"What?"

"Don't. Don't do this. You don't need to do this."

"I don't understand."

"Just leave it beautiful," Hannah says.

She's at the end of the bridge. But how could she be? She takes a step towards you. Part of you wants to run to her and throw your arms around her and not let go. But how could she be here? This is not real. Hannah is not in the mountains. She is not here. Close your eyes. Open them slowly. Slowly.

Jesus! Hannah! She's standing there unsure. Tense. There's an edgy sustained high note in her body. And Frannie? What does she see?

"What are you doing here?" you whisper. Did you speak this out loud? Did it make it into the air?

Frannie is silent beside you.

It's Hannah who speaks.

"Remember how when we walked it was as if we were the same person? Our hips would fit together somehow. What about making love? Do you remember our love making? My god, we fucked like crazy rabbits. Beautiful desire."

"Yes, but…"

"Remember the good things."

"I do remember the good things. But I think there's something else."

"Yes," she says moving a few steps closer. "There's the pain of stopping. We stopped. I went away. I'm sorry."

"Why? Why are you sorry?"

"Because I caused you pain."

"I always knew we were heading in that direction. I convinced myself that it was worth it."

"And?"

"And there's something wrong."

"I miss you. I miss your touch. How you defined my body as something loved."

"Life goes on."

"Yes," she says. "It surely does."

You remember it was a beautiful meshing on the night she told you. There were candles, too many to count. You lit candles. You remember the smoothness of her skin in candlelight. The tones. And the temperature in the small bedroom increased dramatically. It became a small, amorous cathedral.

You were gods that night. Invincible.

And when she told you, she cried, and you were unable. You could not cry.

"And you sent 51 poems," she says. She is sitting up on the bridge railing, her feet dangling above the water.

"You counted?"

"Yes. I grew to rely on them. They became an essential element of my days, of my weeks. They were pills against reality."

"There were supposed to be fifty-two."

"I figured as much."

"I didn't write the last one."

"Very romantic to not let the seduction end, to not finish."

"No, not romantic. Perhaps it was a turning away from arriving. Perhaps the journey towards you became more important than arriving."

Hannah smiles softly.

"Perhaps the last poem would have been…different," you say.

"It's perfect that it doesn't exist."

"It would not have been pretty, I think."

Sadness descends on this image of Hannah. Grief falls into her and fills her to the brim. She begins to look lost, unsure. "I had to. I had no choice…. It was the only sane thing to do."

"Choice," you say.

Frannie stirs beside you. She's shivering. "What?" she says.

You wrap your arm around her more tightly.

"Nothing."

"You said something."

"Did I?"

You look down the bridge and there is no one there. You'd like to go down there and check for footprints. See if she left a scent.

See if there's a hint of anything real. But you don't move.

⊱—○—⊰

Will this sudden ceremony of letting go on the bridge make everything better? Is this physical letting go a solution to your frenzy? No, it is simply a letting go. It is what it is. Human beings want to be so goddamned complicated. They, ha, we, say we want simplicity but with each passing year, more and more stuff piles up. There is probably great happiness in a simple uncluttered life.

⊱—○—⊰

What if at some subconscious level, you're waiting for her? You're waiting for a call, a letter, a telegram. You'll put all your heart, all your craving into Frannie but there is a small part of you that waits. You do not expect to ever see Hannah again. You do not have that expectation. You do not even have that hope but there is something in you that waits. There are times in your life when you wish for her company. There are times when you think only of her. Is that alright? Is it alright to think: *she'd have liked this,* occasionally?

Dropping that sheet of paper into the stream might allow you to love outside of Hannah. It might allow you to move on with your life. It creates space. By saying good-bye to the unwritten poem you have given yourself space, but not peace. Not yet.

There is the distinct possibility that you will have to write that last poem someday.

Hannah left. She denied a life together by her actions. And her actions were sane, and understandable, and reasonable. Perhaps you were expecting insanity from her. There is nothing to forgive. And there is nothing to forget. Ah, but that's not true. There is something you'd like to forget.

⊱—○—⊰

But what if being with someone is not an ownership? What if it's an engagement of life together? You bring the best of yourself and engage in life together, grow together. We all have pasts. We all come with history.

⊱⊰

There's a hammock strung up outside Frannie's cabin, on the verandah. On cool spring mornings you and Frannie read in the hammock, bodies pushed together under a quilt, coffee pot within reach. Occasionally, you'll add the Irish Cream liqueur to your coffee.

On a morning in May, with the clouds down around your ankles and a persistent drizzle you are reading one of Frannie's books: Thomas Moore's *Soul Mates.* Moore says relationships do not demand that we surrender to another person, but rather "that we acknowledge a soul in which the parties are mingled and respect its unpredictable demands."

⊱⊰

When you drop the sheet of paper into the water it catches the orange of the sunset, a flutter in your eye, and then it's in the stream of water. It's inside the water that descends from Lake Cavell. The water takes it, holds it for a few seconds near the top of the current and then smoothly swallows it.

⊱⊰

When you look up at Frannie, you know there is a new freedom. If someone were building a puzzle of this scene, one of the pieces in between you and Frannie just clicked into place. It's by no means a complete picture but you can suddenly see her eyes are green. Her eyes are green. There's a small scar beside her left eye—a faint curved sliver of moon.

sixteen

Frannie

You do not push her. She looks at you when you are back in the car with the heater blasting and the first stars poking through the darkness. It's her idea.

"There's something I need to do." She opens the car door.

"Do you want me there?"

"No," she says. "Something I have to do alone."

Frannie pulls a tattered *Selected Alpine Climbs* from her coat pocket. She takes a deep breath and opens the car door. You shut off the car. An astounding silence enfolds you as you watch her move towards the bridge. You know whose book that is. You found it on the shelf in the cabin. It has his name in it.

Before she pushes the door shut, Frannie leans into the car and kisses your face. "Give me five minutes. Then bring the flask."

Moonlight smears the clouds behind Cavell. It's cold. You see Frannie hesitate, hug herself. You know it is colder on the bridge, above the water.

"It's hard," she says, quiet as snow. "He loved this book."

It's just a symbolic act, you think. That's all it is. You're not denying love, or memory, or resolve for either of those things.

You're simply saying the past is the past, the present is where you are now, and the future is a brilliant unknown thing.

"You don't have to do this," you say.

"Yes, I do."

She holds it there above the water, her hand shaking a little. She closes her eyes.

Who can account for the absurdity of human memory? A series of images begins to flicker through Frannie's mind like a drug-induced spastic 16mm film projector. It starts with the drop away of the cornice. She was turned away from the accident. She had to flip her body around to see a flash of colour and white. She would have given her own life, everything, anything, for his eyes. The steady blue-gray eyes. Forgiveness? Perhaps there would have been forgiveness in them, love. Perhaps a peaceful resignation to the facts. And the sound. A dull thud. She was moving so slowly. There's no way she could have said anything. And the sky was so blue. Once the three and the cornice dropped to the bottom there was the pissing blue sky. Alberta is famous for its clear blue skies.

And then she sees him pacing the rooms and hallways of their house getting ready for a climb. Bob always paced before a climb, adding and subtracting items from his pack, and hers. Fretting about the route. Checking the weather. Going over old climbing journals. Looking at the topos.

And then she feels his body pressed against hers. And his face. His face, she can see his face. His eyes, and hair, tawny and wild. A narrow face, always, it seemed, with an odd tan. He always had stripes of some kind on his face from sunglasses, or goggles, or a sloppy application of sunscreen.

And there he is at the Chickadee with maps spread out on the table and a bottle of wine. And he looks so happy. Happy to have the wine and the maps and to have the prospect of climbing.

Frannie lets the book drop from her hand into the dark current. Her hand goes limp, hangs down like it's dead. She inhales quickly as if she's made a horrible mistake. The book vanishes in a blink, even before it hits the water. There is only the constant sound of the rushing water as it disappears. A molecular strand of her consciousness wants her to jump into the water and retrieve the book, or is it to be with him. She doesn't know but dismisses this half impulse and turns toward you.

⋈

Then you are alone with Frannie in the front seat of the car, with snow beginning to dot the windshield and the heater belching. It's always snowing somewhere in the mountains, you think.

⋈

By considering one thing perhaps you automatically admit the exigent possibility of its opposite?

⋈

Is this where you stay? Is this it? Perhaps you should go back to the city and figure out how to heal, alone. But how could you possibly consider leaving Frannie? She is not what you settle for because you cannot have what you want. You know this. This is an extraordinary woman. There is hope and love with Frannie. Where would you go anyway? You're not going east to seek out Hannah are you? Why? Why would you seek out a denial of life? Perhaps you're going west to find the nun. The nun with such temerity and courage. That makes sense for you. She's yet another unavailable woman.

⋈

What if you never meet Hannah again? But that isn't the issue is it? What if you stop feeling that you want to meet her again? You make a decision somewhere along the line that regardless of your lingering feelings, you've finished with this woman. And the years move like those glaciers and ice fields that have become fixtures of your landscape. Time pulverizes your memories into a fine powder, a silt that is only beautiful when mixed with clear water. And then it becomes a murky turquoise thickness in mountain lakes. Years from now, you'll be in the mountains with your daughter and she'll ask you why the lakes are that strange colour.

"Because they hold beautiful memories," you'll say.

"Oh," your daughter will say, as if it's become perfectly clear to her.

"It's the memories mixed with the cold water, and the warm sun," you add, more for yourself than anybody. And then you'll pick her up and continue walking along the edge of that lake. I've become a periphery to my own memories, you'll think. And then you'll wish your daughter love. A series of hopes will move through you silently. They will appear as prayers. You hope that she feels love intensely. And that she loses love intensely. That she feels everything before and in between and after. That she is able to be present through it all. That she will remember this moment—that she will remember that the cool murky green colour of mountain lakes is caused by beautiful memories.

(51)
huddled in dim light

huddled together in dim light
bathed in the cool autumn air
the curves of your face are a string quartet
playing gently, softly like small water
I am overfilled, spilled, requiemed with feeling
It's as if I do not know who you are
after everything we have done
after seeing you in so many possible lights
this extraordinary glimpse of yet another stranger
astounds beautifully
me

It does not happen immediately. It does not happen the next day. It does not happen the next week. Three weeks go by and then one morning you wake up and notice it. Not peace. Not contentment. But rather, there is a lack of restlessness in you.

You wake up in the cabin and Frannie is there beside you. The room is cool with the morning. You get up and start the fire that you prepared the night before. You crawl back in beside Frannie. Look around the small cabin. Two shelves of books. Several stacks of books on the floor. The old dulled-silver espresso maker on the stove. Something smells like vanilla. A candle? The fire begins to crackle. It throws its own light into the room, fills in details where the morning has yet to reach.

In a few minutes you'll get up and put the espresso on, perhaps adjust the fire. The room begins to warm, but it is not something you notice. There's a slow seeping of heat into the room. Then Nick might knock on the door. He often comes by for his first coffee of the day. He likes your thick, black style of coffee.

Maybe this morning, you won't wake Frannie. You'll let Nick in, pour coffee and then you'll both go out on the deck. You'll sit in the big-armed wooden chairs. Perhaps this morning you'll say something about how you were wondering if Nick could use a hand around the place. You might say that you'll understand if he says no. You're looking for a place to write and work. Best to perform some sort of physical labour so that when you come to the writing, you're fresh. Then you might look at his face and see in his eyes he is pleased. He might have tilted his head slightly like someone who knows the answer to a question long before it's posed.

And Nick might surprise you by saying: "Well, it's about time." And then he'll pull out a couple of Monte Cristo Number 4s and insist that you join him. "A good cigar for the morning," he'll say. And so you'll sit and smoke in silence. Drink your coffee and smoke in the morning light.

What if nothing happens? What if you sit across from each other in a cafe and feel nothing. Outside it's drizzling and cold. You and Hannah talk for a few hours and…nothing. Too much denial of life has become an insurmountable wall. You drink a bottle of wine. You notice a few more wrinkles. The waiter makes googily eyes at you because he thinks the two of you should be in love. That, at least, hasn't changed. Waiters were always doing things for you when you were…but that's the past. Hannah notices a little less hair. You drink another bottle of wine. But there is no lovely connection. You do not fall into a timeless lovemaking with violins and skin and countless kisses. This yearning has been fruitless. All that time. All that hesitant craving. The thing that is never looked at directly. The thing that was never finished. And nothing. Nothing. You get up and shake hands, almost hug, say awkward good-byes outside the restaurant and that's it. She's in a cab and down the street. And you're standing there with a penetrating eastern chill going right through you.